QUEST FOR
PLANET X

TESSA GRATTON

ILLUSTRATIONS BY
PETUR ANTONSSON

DISNEP

LUCASFILM
PRESS

LOS ANGELES·NEW YORK

Printed in the United States of America

First Edition, April 2023

10 9 8 7 6 5 4 3 2 1

FAC-058958-23048

ISBN 978-1-368-08287-7

Library of Congress Control Number on file

Reinforced binding

Design by Soyoung Kim and Scott Piehl

Visit the official *Star Wars* website at: www.starwars.com.

STAR WARS
THE HIGH REPUBLIC

QUEST OF THE JEDI

There is conflict in the galaxy. Chaos on the Pilgrim Moon of Jedha has resulted in a devastating battle. In its aftermath, the Jedi have learned of the involvement of the seemingly benevolent group THE PATH OF THE OPEN HAND in violent interplanetary conspiracies.

With communications down, the leader of the Path, THE MOTHER, races back to the planet Dalna to make her ultimate escape.

Little do the Jedi know that the Mother is about to unleash mysterious, nameless creatures with the power to destroy the Order once and for all....

STAR WARS TIMELINE

THE HIGH REPUBLIC

FALL OF THE JEDI

REIGN OF THE EMPIRE

THE PHANTOM MENACE

ATTACK OF THE CLONES

THE CLONE WARS

REVENGE OF THE SITH

THE BAD BATCH

SOLO: A STAR WARS STORY

OBI-WAN KENOBI

AGE OF REBELLION

REBELS

ANDOR

ROGUE ONE:
A STAR WARS
STORY

A NEW HOPE

THE EMPIRE
STRIKES BACK

RETURN OF
THE JEDI

THE NEW REPUBLIC

THE BOOK
OF BOBA FETT

THE
MANDALORIAN

RISE OF THE FIRST ORDER

RESISTANCE

THE FORCE
AWAKENS

THE LAST JEDI

THE RISE OF
SKYWALKER

"**B**eware the Jedi," Er Dal said to his partner Fel Ix as he buckled the straps of Fel Ix's leather gauntlet around his gray left wrist.

They stood in their family quarters deep in the belly of the *Gaze Electric*, tucked beneath the central hall of worship along with the rest of the members of the Path of the Open Hand. The ship had been a good home to Fel Ix and his family. It was all long lines and jagged edges, with streaks of bright blue here and there. Alone in a pocket of the frontier without any charted hyperspace lanes, the starship cut silently through the galaxy like a huge, sleek shark. But as dangerous as the warship looked, it kept them safe, and Fel Ix was reluctant to say goodbye.

He and his family were Kessarine, from a swampy planet in the Outer Rim, and since the day Fel Ix had met his partners, Er Dal and Ferize, he had never left them. For the past three years they had lived on the small planet Dalna, making a home with the Path of the Open Hand. They had been happy and safe enough to have their first clutch of babies only a month earlier. But the leader of the Path, the Mother, had a vision of the Path traveling throughout the galaxy, fighting to keep the Force free, and the Mother was sending Fel Ix on an important mission of his own.

"Er Dal speaks truly," said their other partner, Ferize. "Beware the Jedi. You will certainly encounter them."

Silently, Er Dal and Fel Ix faced her. She sat on a low sofa, their newly hatched babies curled on her lap in various states of sleep. Ferize smiled grimly at Fel Ix, who knelt beside the babies and carefully picked up the little one called Fe Fer. The baby's tiny scales were beginning to show along the edges of his miniature cheek frills, and Fel Ix nuzzled his child, wishing he could remain with his family. But the Mother had chosen Fel Ix for this mission specifically. It was an honor to be chosen by their spiritual leader, and as much as Fel Ix loved his family, they wanted him to go. They believed in the Path of the Open Hand. They trusted the Mother. Wasn't the Path their family, too?

After putting Fe Fer into Er Dal's hands, Fel Ix leaned toward Ferize. He let his cheek furls touch hers, feeling the tension in them, and his own. Fel Ix breathed deeply. He hissed and popped in Kessarine, "I know you will be well without me."

"Well, but not happy," Ferize hissed and popped back. The language of their home planet allowed them to speak in either air or water. A long time before, his people had been amphibious, but now they could not breathe underwater. Their green or gray skin still had tiny scales in places, their cheek and head furls looked like sea kelp, and they still had an inner set of eyelids to protect their eyes, as well as three strong tails. Fel Ix kept his tails wrapped around his waist and thighs when he had to wear a jumpsuit instead of Path robes.

"The Force will be free," Er Dal said in Galactic Basic. It was one of the mottos of the Path of the Open Hand.

They believed that the Force should not be used, and tried to live in harmony with its will. Er Dal raised a long-fingered greenish hand and tugged affectionately on one of Fel Ix's cheek frills. He said, "It is an honor to help the Mother's mission. Especially after . . ."

"Yes," Fel Ix said. Er Dal meant the battle on the moon Jedha the day before. The battle had been violent and scary, especially because it had begun during peace talks involving all kinds of people who believed in the power of the Force. But the Jedi had fought against the Path, and the Mother had unleashed the glowing blue creature she called the Leveler. The Leveler had defeated the Jedi and returned balance to the Force, but not before one of the great stone statues of Jedha fell. And even worse, the Path's Herald—a strong Nautolan who used to share the role of leadership with the Mother—had betrayed them and been left behind on Jedha. The whole situation was uncomfortable and frightening. But they trusted the Mother to take care of them.

Fel Ix stood. He blinked his inner and outer eyelids as he studied his immediate family, curled together and soft-looking in their gray-and-blue Path robes. Fel Ix opened his hands, palms up, and bowed. "The Force will be free," he said. Then he left their quarters.

As Fel Ix moved out of the living space of the *Gaze Electric*, the wide-open rooms and spacious corridors with their soft curtains and blue-and-gray decorations gave way to the more battle-ready parts of the warship. Stark black walls blinked with lights, and the corridors narrowed with purpose. The hum of the ship engine caused Fel Ix's cheek tendrils to tremble.

He reached a juncture that led in one direction toward the bridge and observation decks and in the other toward the docking bay. Waiting for him were the Mother herself and Fel Ix's friend Marda Ro.

Marda was Fel Ix's favorite person outside of his family. She was Evereni and nearly his age, with deep black eyes, cold gray skin, and the sharp teeth of a predator. But instead of taking after so many of her people, Marda was loyal and gentle. She had helped his babies break out of their eggs only a few weeks earlier, and saved their lives. Fel Ix wanted her to be their friend, too, when they grew up.

Neither Marda nor the Mother spoke, simply waiting for Fel Ix to arrive. The Mother was a human woman with dark brown skin and warm eyes, in the voluptuous robes of the Path Elders. Despite her recent injuries, to Fel Ix she was beautiful and exuded charm and comfort. It was easy to believe the Force had chosen her to be its spokesperson, especially with the Leveler always at her side. The creature frightened and inspired Fel Ix with its power. He tore his gaze away from its creepy eyes and looked back at Marda. Marda was still. Her black hair was braided softly around her face, and she wore the long gray-and-blue robes all the Path used to wear when they lived on the planet Dalna as farmers and simple gatherers—before the Mother had brought them to the stars in the *Gaze Electric*. She smiled at Fel Ix. Three bright blue lines of brikal-shell paint cut starkly down over her eyes and nose. It was strange: Marda used to wear her paint in soft waves on her forehead, but now her lines were bolder.

In her hands she held a shallow bowl of brikal-shell blue paint.

Fel Ix stopped before them and bowed again, his palms up. When he straightened, Marda smiled. "Allow me?" she said softly.

"Always," Fel Ix answered, stepping closer. Marda

dipped three long fingers into the blue paint and reached out to touch them against Fel Ix's forehead. She streaked the paint in three hard angles. "Go with freedom, harmony, and clarity," she said.

"The Force will be free," Fel Ix murmured in return.

To clean her hand, Marda smeared the last of the blue against his shoulder armor. It made Fel Ix smile.

"You're clear about the mission?" the Mother asked in her rich voice. Her smile was mild.

"Yes, Mother. I have the map of priority buoys, and I memorized the characters of the Graffian slicer code so that I don't have to have any physical copies."

"Impressive," the Mother murmured.

Fel Ix bowed again, and remained with his head lowered.

Marda said, "I'll walk you to your ship."

The Mother said, "Be quick and light, Fel Ix, and return to us." She briefly touched his temple, then turned to head back toward the bridge, footsteps echoing off the dark walls. Once she had vanished into the throat of the *Gaze Electric*, Marda moved nearer to Fel Ix. She bumped her shoulder against his and then gestured for him to go with her. The silly shoulder bump reminded him of how young they both were, despite all they'd done and the families they'd built.

Fel Ix followed easily, studying his friend. The pattern of her brikal-shell lines was not the only thing that had changed. Though she still found smiles for Fel Ix, she carried herself more coldly and confidently than before—before the Jedi, before the battle on Jedha. Fel Ix hoped she was only growing up, not growing mean. Fel Ix's partner Ferize worried that this struggle between the Path and the Jedi would hollow out Marda's heart. But Fel Ix had faith that Marda would serve the Path and the Force with determination, and he wanted to do the same. The Force needed to be free, and they would fight to make it so.

As they walked down one of the slowly curving corridors that led into the lower levels of the ship, Fel Ix and Marda passed other Path members going about their business—new business. Everyone but the children and the most elderly worked to maintain the *Gaze Electric*, to hone weapons and keep the starship in order. Other teams were preparing to depart, too, though Fel Ix did not know the nature of those missions. He willed his cheek frills to be calm and limp, a neutral expression for Kessarine. Not that most people could read Kessarine expressions. But Marda had spent enough time with them to know. He didn't want her to think he was nervous.

They reached the hangar bay, a long but narrow bay lined with seven different small ships and shuttles, half of them marked with the blue of the Path, while the others had no distinguishing features other than identification numbers stenciled on their noses. Fel Ix's was one of the unmarked ships, a sleek little shuttle they'd fitted out for long voyages. It carried only three crew members, including him.

Marda stopped at the entrance to the bay. Fel Ix paused with her, turning. "Marda?"

She smiled, and it was her new, hungrier smile. The one with teeth. Fel Ix let his cheek frills stretch in an answering smile. Then he said, "Take care of my Littles."

Surprisingly, Marda glanced away. But before Fel Ix could ask what was wrong, she looked right into his eyes with her huge black ones. "I will hold their names in my heart, in harmony with the Force," she said. Then she leaned closer. "But I am unsure I'll be with them."

"What?"

Marda took his wrist. "I have a mission of my own."

Fel Ix nodded. "The Force will be free."

"Exactly." Marda grinned again. Then her expression slipped back into seriousness. "But, Fel Ix, I wanted to warn you . . ."

He waited. Droid beeps, the hiss of soldering lasers, and raised voices—regular sounds of a hangar bay—surrounded them. The new sounds of the Path of the Open Hand.

"The Jedi," Marda said darkly. "After Jedha . . ." She shook her head. "More of them will come. The Mother is *ready*, and your mission is part of that readiness. But you're leaving the safety of her open hands. Be careful. Be wary. They are dangerous."

Fel Ix held out his hands, palms up. He fought a chill, because Marda and his partners echoed each other's fears. Slowly Marda placed her cool hands underneath his, palms to his scaled knuckles. He said, "I will serve the will of the Force. I am not afraid of the Jedi."

TWO

Jedi Padawan Rooper Nitani had spent most of her time on Batuu in the archive at the Jedi research facility located a short speeder's drive from Black Spire Outpost.

She didn't mind all the research—there was so much to learn in the journals and holobooks that had been collected from around the frontier. After her adventures on Gloam with her master, Silandra Sho, Rooper understood that it never hurt to be prepared with as much information as possible before diving into the sorts of situations Jedi frequently found themselves in.

On her second day in the archive, she'd even been rewarded for her diligence. She didn't like to think of it as a reward, because that made it sound like she was owed something. The Force did not owe anyone anything. The Jedi did not expect rewards. Perhaps it was more of a gift. She'd been walking down a long line of artifacts from the Outer Rim, studying the strange shapes as she practiced categorizing them into classes. Suddenly, Rooper heard her name whispered.

She whirled but saw nothing. Nobody was in the artifact chamber with her.

Looking around, Rooper had centered herself with the Force. She saw the Force as colors: bright rainbows and glowing rays, the colors reflecting names and needs and, she thought, the will of the Force. When Rooper closed her eyes, the chamber flared brightly in splotchy brilliance because everything there was connected to the Force. But one thing hummed a cool pink, beckoning her. It was a small compass tucked behind the crystalized skull of an ancient Batuu sea bear. Rooper had touched it and felt calm.

When she explained it to Master Merak, the dedicated

archivist at the temple outpost, the old Gran had blinked all three of his eyes consecutively and suggested she put the compass in her pocket—continue listening to the Force. So that's what Rooper had done.

But today she was very distracted from her studies and listening. Rumors had reached them of some kind of battle or conflict on the moon Jedha, and Rooper's master, Silandra Sho, was there. Silandra had always wanted to visit Jedha for a pilgrimage, and even though Rooper would love to visit there someday, too—to see the ancient statues and the Temple of the Kyber or meet Force users who weren't even Jedi!—it hadn't felt like the right time for Rooper yet. Some things a Jedi had to do on her own. So Silandra had left Rooper with Master Merak and traveled alone to Jedha.

The rumors from Jedha were wild and thin—but they were all anyone on Batuu was talking about. They said violence had broken out and that many different believers and followers of the Force had been involved, including the Jedi! Maybe one of those ancient statues had fallen, and unbelievably, there'd been a monster? Some kind of monster that caused all sorts of chaos. Nobody had any real news—not even Master Merak. Rooper wanted to jump on a shuttle and fly to her master on Jedha immediately. She couldn't, of course. Her duty was on Batuu, for now.

She felt it, though, that something was gathering out there on the frontier, and it was dangerous enough the Jedi had turned most of their attention toward it. Rooper wanted to help! But to help, she needed information. For once, the information couldn't be found in the archive. She needed real-time accounts. Official transmissions. She'd even take rumors and speculation if they led her toward answers. Or a mission.

But Master Merak told her to be patient. The Force would provide, and until then she was safe.

Frustrated as Rooper was, she spent only a few early hours reading in the rotunda of the archive before running through meditations and exercises with her lightsabers. She grabbed a couple of spiced cloud-cricket fritters instead of full lunch, because she was heading into Black Spire Outpost that afternoon and there was so much street food there to fill her up. She'd buy a meal to share with her friend Dass Leffbruk before he left for the Hyperspace

Chase with his father the next morning. Maybe he'd heard different rumors about Jedha!

Finally, she left the white-stone Jedi temple as the Batuu suns cast long afternoon shadows. The temple towers rose like fingers among the ancient petrified trees that marred the brilliant green forest. The trees looked like huge towers themselves, which was how the outpost got the name Black Spire. Rooper did like Batuu quite a lot. The Force bound all life together, and on a planet so lush with life, everything looked to Rooper like a beautiful blurry melting pot. And the spires of Batuu, even though they were long dead and long petrified, swarmed with bugs and moss and still shone with the Force when Rooper reached out.

They comforted her, almost as much as the towers of the temple did, because they mirrored the crown of the main Jedi Temple on Coruscant.

The weather that day was pleasant but chilly as a slow wind blew rain in from the sea. Rooper had on her dark brown cloak, the hood hanging over her shoulders. Her utility belt was tied around her blue Padawan sash, and she had some additional utility pouches strapped to her thighs over her tall boots. Of course her twin blue lightsabers were holstered on either hip. She'd just turned fifteen about a week before and felt very grown-up alone out there.

Rooper made her way from the temple toward Black Spire Outpost. Pretty songs from mud frogs filled the air, and a few shrieking scalemonks swung in the living trees. It wasn't long before she saw the first of the flat domes that marked the mudbrick and limestone buildings of Black Spire.

She hoped Dass would be ready to spend time with her. He was a few years younger than Rooper, but they'd bonded on their escape from Gloam. Dass was a nervous kid but had proved himself brave when necessary. Rooper admired that and found it really interesting when he started talking about all the trouble he and his family had gotten into as hyperspace prospectors. Dass had been born on a long prospecting journey, in between short jumps, he'd told her once—though of course that was just a story his dad had told him to help him remember his mom.

Rooper would miss Dass when he and his father, Spence, left Batuu the next morning. They'd contracted with the San Tekka family to lease a ship and join in something called the Hyperspace Chase. It was a contest of some sort to route hyperspace lanes, sponsored by the San Tekkas and the Grafs, two families with deep ties to the frontier. The prospectors competed to map the safest routes through hyperspace, to the best places, and earned the right to sell them to either family. Reputations and plenty of credits could be made. Dass had told Rooper he hoped they could use the San Tekkas' ship to reach the mysterious planet called Planet X. Most people thought the planet was a myth, made up by wild-eyed prospectors who'd been driven mad by deep space or who liked spinning fantastic stories. But Rooper was one of only a handful of people who knew that Dass and his dad had actually been there. They'd crash-landed their ship, the *Silverstreak*, on Planet X and barely escaped with their lives. Then they'd been betrayed by their awful partner and had no proof of their voyage. Dass was very excited to get back there and reclaim the *Silverstreak*.

Rooper had a bad feeling about all of it but wished Dass good luck.

The whole point of the Hyperspace Chase seemed backward to her, anyway. Rooper thought hyperspace should be public, not private, and overseen by the Republic, but not everybody agreed. Opening up the frontier was one of the reasons she and Master Silandra had been working with a Republic Pathfinder team until recently. The Pathfinder teams aimed to make life better for the residents of the Outer Rim. They brought healers and communications and justice along with them.

Picking up her pace, Rooper waved at a bright yellow Mikkian woman with matching yellow head tendrils that snaked around her head. The Mikkian was selling little jars of refreshing juice and green and blue milk right beyond the massive arching gate that led into Black Spire. Rooper headed directly toward the spaceport, where Dass and his dad were staying at a travelers' hostel until their transport arrived to take them to the starting lineup for the Hyperspace Chase.

Rooper couldn't help worrying about Dass and the risks of hyperspace prospecting. It was dangerous work, charting brand-new routes around gravity wells and to unknown solar systems, while possibly running straight into comet chains or space debris. But Dass wanted to get back to Planet X to retrieve their ship, no matter the danger. Dass said the planet was full of strange creatures and twisted, beautiful flora. The potential was endless. The descriptions sounded incredible. Rooper would love to see it herself! Prospectors had been searching for the legendary planet for years, at least the few who believed it existed. The stories started with an early prospector named Xirys Patri, who claimed to have crashed there and barely made it out with a handful of riches—miraculously healed of his life-threatening injuries. The riches had been unlike anything anyone had seen before, precious and beautiful. Dass had loved telling Rooper the story. He wanted to discover a planet of his own someday.

Dass and his dad—and their awful former partner, Sunshine Dobbs—had been the first people to find Planet X again since Xirys. They'd managed to navigate through a weird storm surrounding the planet and proved the old rumors true: Planet X was real. Their ship crashed, and they barely escaped. But on the way home, Sunshine had stolen the routes to the hidden planet and stranded the two Leffbruks on the planet Gloam. Dass and Spence had almost died alone on Gloam, at the mercy of ancient Katikoot inhabitants who'd been transformed into monsters. Only the arrival of the Jedi had helped them escape.

This Hyperspace Chase was the perfect opportunity for Dass and his dad to retrieve the *Silverstreak*. By agreeing to represent the San Tekkas in the race, Spence was getting a prospecting ship with all the required tech and beacons. And the San Tekkas were glad to help—even though most people thought the legends about Planet X were either fake or exaggerated, Spence and Dass's experience with Planet X had revitalized the rumors about it and gotten a lot more people excited to pay their entry fees into the Chase.

Even though Rooper had a bad feeling, she was glad to see Dass eager to get back out there. He'd been so afraid on Gloam that almost anything was worth the spark of excitement that was back in his eyes.

Before Rooper made the last turn toward the hostel, she stopped at a food stall and bought two skewers of sweet roasted spire acorns. They weren't really acorns but chunks of a soft rootwood that had been soaked and then cooked. Rooper knew Dass loved them.

Carrying the skewers in one hand, she shaded her eyes

from the last rays of the second sun as it winked behind one of the massive spires that split the nearest building in two.

Just then, she felt an eddy in the Force, disrupting its regular flow. She turned around in time to notice some people in the crowd along the wide road leading toward the spaceport shifting on their feet and frowning. A Shistavanen with huge furred ears flattened them back. The crowd parted, and there was Dass Leffbruk, running full tilt.

His panicked green eyes lit up when he saw Rooper.

"Rooper!" he cried, waving a gangly arm as he ran. "There you are!"

"Dass?" Rooper let her free hand fall to the pommel of one of her lightsabers.

Dass skidded to a stop in front of her. "You've got to help! My friend is being attacked by pirates!"

Rooper ran after Dass, heart pounding.

Dass darted ahead of her, dodging people. It was even more crowded closer to the spaceport, and Rooper frowned as she concentrated. She wished she could take time to stop and yell for people to make way, but if she did that, she'd lose Dass.

He turned left into a less crowded alley between a mechanic's shop and a run-down trade storefront. Rooper could breathe a little better and reached out to grab Dass's jacket. "Hey," she said, tugging him to a stop.

Dass turned and nearly tripped on a pile of wires

spilling out from a discarded droid torso that leaned against the mechanic's shop wall. "Sorry, but Sky is alone, and there are three of these big goons trying to force their way onto the ship."

"Who?"

"My friend Sky—their ship, pirates are trying to steal it, or take them, or something!"

"Why didn't you get the constabulary? There's a Republic frontier office right in the spaceport."

Dass shook his head. He grabbed her hand and started running again. Rooper didn't fight it, following him quickly. As they came out of the alley, Dass said, "No time. I'd have to convince them somehow. But I knew you'd just *help* me."

Rooper felt a little pleased warmth in her chest and tried to push it down. It was good for a Jedi to be known as helpful but not to be known as a pushover. She said, "Okay."

They'd taken the alley shortcut behind the main spaceport, to where several landing pads were lined up like bantha stalls between the rough spires. Most of the spaces held ships, and Dass pulled Rooper past the first landing pad, with its beat-up old transport shuttle, to the next, which housed a very shiny, very expensive-looking silver-and-black minicruiser. Sure enough, three large, mean-looking goons stood below the sharp nose of the ship. A big white-skinned human with a laser rifle strapped across his back and the tallest Lutrillian Rooper had ever seen flanked the leader: another human, this one with multicolored ribbons wound into her hair, too pretty to match the scarred black armor that covered her body.

"Let us in, kid," the leader said. Her voice was loud and firm but not quite a yell.

The Lutrillian glanced over his shoulder at Rooper and Dass's arrival but only flicked a spiked ear and returned his attention to the ship. They'd been dismissed. Rooper clenched her jaw. She was young, and not everybody on the frontier recognized Jedi, but it was still rude.

"Leave the *Brightbird* alone!" Dass yelled. He stood just behind Rooper, but with his hands on his hips and his chin up aggressively. "Or we'll make you!"

"Dass," Rooper cautioned gently. She needed a better handle on what exactly was going on. Dass had really just tossed her into the deep end of the saltwater tank.

All three goons turned to face them and eyed Rooper up and down. The human man swung his blaster rifle off his shoulder and lazily leaned against it, the muzzle pressed to the ground. It was a clear threat.

"Make us?" the leader said, affecting surprise on her tan face.

"I am Jedi Padawan Rooper Nitani," Rooper said. She drew herself taller, as if she had any authority in the situation. "If you wouldn't mind, what are you doing harassing the owner of this ship?"

The Lutrillian snorted, but the leader of the goons smirked prettily. "Owner? I assure you the owner of this ship simply wants it back. That's my job. No reason for the *Jedi* to get involved."

The way she said *Jedi* gave it a lot of weight—but Rooper wasn't sure it was good weight. She cleared her throat. "If you have an issue with who owns this ship, shouldn't it be taken up with the planetary authorities? The Republic's Office of the Frontier—"

"We don't want to trouble everyone with officials," the human woman said smoothly. She let her hand fall to her hip, thumb touching the handle of a small blaster.

Rooper kept her eyes on the goons, but with her next exhale she let her awareness of the Force spread out. She could feel Dass's anxiety spiking orange next to her, and the tension between the goons pulled everything tight. If Master Silandra were there, what would she do? Rooper had to say something. She smiled thinly. "I think if the current occupant of the ship doesn't want to let you in, an official report is the only polite way to proceed."

"Polite?" the human man grumbled. He drummed his fingers on the butt of his rifle. "Do we look like the polite sort to you?"

"Well, I am the polite sort," Rooper said. Her hands itched to fall to her lightsabers, just for comfort, and she suddenly remembered she was still holding two skewers of roasted acorns! A tiny grimace pinched her mouth, and the goon leader saw it.

The human woman grinned.

Rooper tried to get a handle on the situation. "What does the current occupant of the ship have to say? Have they responded to you?"

"We tried to get the kid to come down," said the Lutrillian.

A kid? Rooper thought. *Oh, no.*

The human leader reached up to rap her gloved knuckles hard against the silver underbelly of the ship. "Knock, knock, kid," she called. She was looking right at a swiveling sensor with a convex lens that had to be a camera. "Come on out and face us."

"Eat rocks, slimeball," the ship said in a very young-sounding voice.

The leader turned to Rooper with raised eyebrows as if to say, *See?* Then she wiped all amusement from her expression. "I'm getting in that ship."

Before Rooper could open her mouth, Dass stepped forward.

He said, "Don't you know what a Jedi is? I've seen Rooper take out monsters five times your size without breaking a sweat. I don't think you want to get on her rude side."

Rooper's eyes widened. Dass should not be bragging like that! It was sweet, but he couldn't just throw her at his problems. Especially unprepared. "Dass . . ."

"I do, in fact, know what the Jedi are," the goon leader said. "Which is why you should be helping me reclaim this stolen ship."

Rooper glanced quickly at Dass.

He shook his head, eyes pleading. "I swear, Rooper, this is my friend Sky's ship! It's theirs."

Rooper hesitated. She wanted to trust him. He was her friend. But something was off. Three blaster-armed goons trying to take a very fancy-looking ship away from the person already occupying it? A person who was a kid? Dass wasn't arguing that point, so it might be true. And if there was a kid in the ship, wasn't it right to help them?

Squaring her jaw, Rooper nodded. She had to believe *her* friend. Even if she couldn't see the whole situation, she had to do her best with the information she had. And that meant protecting Dass and his friend.

After a brief pang of regret for missing out on the snack, Rooper dropped the acorn skewers onto the dusty ground. She put both hands on her hips, right beside her lightsabers, and said, much more confidently than she felt, "I'm afraid you'll have to prove it to me at the frontier office, or I won't let you keep harassing Dass's friend."

Both goon minions shifted closer to Rooper, but Rooper didn't move. She didn't unsheathe her lightsabers, either—she wouldn't do that unless she meant to use them, and she really, really hoped she wouldn't have to.

The goon leader stared back at Rooper for a long moment, and then she raised her hands, palms out. "All right, all right. We'll back off."

That was signal enough for the other human and Lutrillian to do so. The human slung his laser rifle back over his shoulder and rolled his eyes. The Lutrillian let out a deep sigh that shook his whiskers.

Rooper backed off a little, nudging Dass's ankle with her toe. He startled, looked at her, then nodded eagerly and stayed at her side as she made room for the goons to leave.

As they did so, the leader winked at Rooper. Some of her ribbons fluttered in a gust of exhaust-stinking wind. Rooper tried not to let any uncertainty show, clenching her jaw to watch them go.

The moment the goons vanished around the farthest of the landing pads, Rooper swallowed a sigh of relief. Dass laughed once, sounding almost panicked, and knocked his fist enthusiastically against her shoulder. They were nearly the same height. Even though he was a few years younger, he was gangly and had grown even more in the couple of months since Gloam.

"That was so great, Rooper!" he said. "You were so impressive! I thought I was going to throw up, but not you! You—"

The sleek silver ship suddenly made a popping sound, and the boarding ramp descended with a hiss.

Dass grabbed her hand. "Yes! You have to meet Sky now, after that! They're inside."

Bewildered, Rooper let herself be dragged up the ramp into the shade of the ship.

CHAPTER FOUR

The moment Rooper and Dass stepped off the ramp and into the little starship, the boarding ramp behind them hissed closed, swallowing them whole. Rooper glanced back, surprised, but she supposed it made sense since those goons could easily return.

The hold was shiny, with polished white plastic and delicate, almost floral black details. They took a sleek spiral staircase to the main deck and a state-of-the-art galley with an elaborate entertainment unit. This ship was definitely a lot fancier than the Pathfinder ships and Jedi shuttles Rooper was used to. Those were practical, functional. This gleamed. She didn't even recognize some of the functions in the galley. There were two exits besides the stairs they'd used: one looked like it led to spacious crew quarters, but Dass took her up a spotless corridor and past pristine, unmarked access panels.

As they walked, Dass kept babbling about how great Rooper was. She winced. It embarrassed her, because she hadn't done anything, really, and leveraging an exaggerated reputation to chase off some goons wasn't exactly the way of the Jedi—she should have pushed for an official solution or run for someone more qualified to mediate, at least. Dass certainly believed this was his friend's ship, but he could've been tricked. Rooper wasn't being responsible.

They reached a cockpit that opened up like a three-petaled flower, a navigation station to one side, communications to the other, and the pilot's berth directly ahead. There sat a teenager who had to be Dass's friend Sky, leaning toward the viewport.

If Rooper had thought the minicruiser gleamed, that was nothing compared with Sky.

"Sky!" Dass greeted.

When Sky swiveled in the pilot's chair, Rooper blinked

at the bright shimmer of the gilded brown-and-gray armored jumpsuit Sky wore. Rays of silver arched across the chest piece like a moonrise, and the rays marked the little caps on their shoulders, too. They looked human, Rooper's age, with peachy skin and thick short hair swept back in black-and-white-striped furrows. Three purple rings pierced their left eyebrow. And when Sky offered Rooper a crooked smile, even their teeth seemed to sparkle expensively.

"Welcome to the *Brightbird*," they said, standing.

"Sky, this is Rooper Nitani, the Jedi I was telling you about. Did you hear how she chased those goons away from your ship?"

"I did. It was impressive." Sky put their hands— covered in piloting gloves made of black material that *also* glittered—on their hips. "Like Dass said, I'm Sky Graf."

They said it like it was supposed to mean more than a name. Rooper blinked, while Dass grinned with pride.

"I'm glad to meet you," Rooper said cautiously.

Sky shrugged, clearly letting go of whatever expectation they'd had about being recognized.

"How do you two know each other?" Rooper thought that seemed like a safe, basic question.

Dass lit up. "I'm joining Sky's crew for the Hyperspace Chase! You should, too!"

Rooper frowned. That was why she should have recognized Sky's name: the Grafs were one of the families sponsoring the Hyperspace Chase. That Dass was signed up for with his dad—not Sky Graf. Rooper said, "Aren't you going with your dad?"

Dass grimaced.

Sky laughed. "I wish I could take you to Mam Possy's for lunch and explanations—I really wanted to get one of those root-worm wraps Dass keeps telling me about. But I think if we leave the *Brightbird*, those slime-eaters will be back and hijack my ship. But I have a fantastic selection of premium teas imported from the Core, and sili juice and some really sharp cheese packs in the galley." Sky gestured with a pretty little bow.

"You aren't going to win me over with the menu," Rooper said lightly, though she thought longingly of the spire acorn skewers gathering dust on the ground outside.

Sky laughed again and leaned closer. "I thought I heard you tell that security punk you were the polite sort?"

Rooper blinked. She pressed her lips together.

"Come on," Sky said, ushering their guests out of the cockpit and down toward the bright galley. A round table with a curving bench that looked like real goldwood— but probably wasn't—was tucked beside the long cabinets marked *cold storage* in Aurebesh.

Dass sat down at the table and gripped his hands together, as if to contain a huge amount of nervous energy. Rooper attempted to sit more gracefully. Sky asked, "Tea?" as they went to put the kettle on. "I'll make my favorite green. It's fifty-seven percent oxidized Orsh Mountain tea, exclusively grown on the seaward-facing cliffs of Orsh Mountain in the northern hemisphere of Chandrila."

Sky threw another smile over their shoulder at Dass and Rooper. "It'll settle all our nerves after your heroics outside."

Rooper wasn't used to being teased like this and didn't think she liked it. But a glance at Dass showed him nodding; so she accepted. While they waited, Dass's knee kept bouncing. He glanced eagerly at Rooper, offering encouraging smiles, but said nothing. It made Rooper nervous—like Dass and Sky had a plan and she was the target.

Instead of letting herself get worked up, Rooper did her

best to breathe deeply and allow the Force to simply flow through her. When they sprang their trap, however wild or silly it turned out to be, Rooper would be ready to counter. And, she thought, maybe this fancy starship would have state-of-the-art comms and Sky would let her reach out to Master Silandra.

When the tea was ready, Sky brought a tray to the fancy table. They slid in beside Dass so the two of them more or less faced Rooper. Sky had added some purple snap chips and a handful of Tarlian candies.

Rooper accepted the tea and took an appreciative sip. It tasted like somebody had set fire to a carefully cultivated orchid farm—in other words, expensive.

Sky and Dass both watched her, and she smiled just a little. The tea was good. "All right," she said. "You promised me answers."

Dass glanced at Sky.

"Fine," Sky said. They sipped their own tea. "I started talking to Dass a few days ago." They glanced at Dass to confirm.

With a mouthful of snap chips, Dass nodded eagerly.

Sky continued, "Grafs—my family—made a lot of our early money in the Core Worlds in shipping and hyperspace-lane trade. Out here on the frontier we've kept it up by mapping our own lanes across various sectors and then charging for the use of our infrastructure."

"Hyperspace lanes should be public," Rooper said, "to promote communication and trade and commerce between systems."

"The competition between my family and the San Tekkas is more lucrative for prospectors," Sky argued. "We wouldn't have half the lanes out here if we left mapping them to the Republic."

Rooper frowned. "Not everybody can afford private lanes. Especially out here. Besides, it's easier for smugglers to have free rein when there aren't even basic official protocols in place."

Sky leaned closer to Rooper. "Isn't that what the Republic sends Jedi for?" they said flirtatiously.

Instead of getting flustered, Rooper narrowed her eyes. "The Republic doesn't *send* Jedi anywhere. It doesn't work like that. We have a council, and we may work with the

Republic and the Office of the Frontier sometimes, but we've been around longer than the Republic and make our own decisions."

"Interesting," Sky said, and Rooper got the feeling they meant it. Sky leaned back, obviously fighting the urge to ask more questions. "So you do understand the necessity of not always letting the Republic make all the decisions. Especially in a place like the Outer Rim where maybe they don't have all the information."

If anything, Rooper managed to narrow her eyes into even more menacing slits. "Tell me what this has to do with Dass joining your team."

"Okay, okay." Sky shot Dass a grin. Dass nodded eagerly again. To Rooper, Sky said, "What do you know about Planet X?"

Rooper shook her head. "Only what Dass has said." She knew from her training it was usually better to let people tell you what they wanted, instead of filling in blanks for them. That way, Sky might reveal more than they meant to.

Sky continued, "There have been rumors about it for so long: that it's paradise, it has trees made of chromium, huge flying fungi, magical healing water, and fields of the most incredible ambrosia, and cloud angels who will grant any wish—you get the idea."

"It's not really like that," Dass said. "But it's gorgeous and . . . alive? Really incredible."

Rooper nodded, and Sky said, "Prospectors have been looking for the route for as long as the rumors have existed, even though nobody ever found anything, or had any evidence. Most people don't believe Planet X exists, and if they do, they don't think that the search is worth the effort. Better to focus on viable hyperspace routes to earn credits than go off on a wild bantha chase. But"—Sky lifted an eyebrow at Rooper conspiratorially—"recently the rumors have resurfaced even more loudly, and one name well-known in prospecting circles has been associated with Planet X: Sunshine Dobbs."

So far, this was all information Rooper already knew. She waited, tight-lipped.

Dass scowled. "Sunshine probably told people that he'd found it on his own, assuming Dad and I died on Gloam. But we didn't!"

"And now Sunshine is making himself scarce and hasn't given anybody the route coordinates," Sky said.

"And Dad is a better prospector than Sunshine ever was," Dass grumbled. "Except since Gloam, he's been so cautious, too cautious. Thanks to Sunshine, he doesn't trust anybody, and I get that—I do!" Dass shook his head, and some of his messy brown hair flopped into his eyes. Rooper had a very older-sister urge to brush it behind his ear, or put him at a desk and make him copy lines until he apologized.

Rooper said, "I thought your dad signed up for the Hyperspace Chase under San Tekka sponsorship?"

Dass looked down. "He did. He wants to get back into prospecting and thinks if he does well enough in the Chase he can earn the ship the San Tekkas are loaning him."

"That's probably accurate," Sky said.

"But why aren't you going with your father?" Rooper struggled to hold back her shock. "Did you argue?"

Dass waved his hands in denial. "No, not really—I mean, yes, but it's because Dad doesn't want to go back to Planet X. He wants to forget we had anything to do with it or with Sunshine. Rooper, our ship is stranded there. The *Silverstreak*. And *we* found the planet first. The routes should be ours to sell. They shouldn't belong to Sunshine

Dobbs or whatever prospector cheats their way to them faster!"

"So you're signing up with another ship? Competing against your dad? Dass!" Rooper wanted to grab him and haul him out of that starship and back to his dad.

"Rooper, please listen." Dass's eyes widened into big round balls of excitement.

Sky put their hand on Dass's shoulder. "I convinced Dass to team up with me. I was making my own plans to use the Hyperspace Chase to look for Planet X, and I heard that sometimes Spence Leffbruk teamed up with Sunshine Dobbs. That's when I realized something everybody else forgot. Dass was with them, too. Just because he's a kid doesn't mean he can't get back there. Dass is a prospector, too."

Dass's face did something funny as he struggled between offense at being called a kid and pride at being called a prospector.

Rooper nodded encouragingly. "That's a good reason to keep working with your dad. Keep learning what he knows."

"Rooper, he doesn't want what I want."

That was an argument Rooper couldn't fully understand. As a Padawan she listened to the Force, but mostly she listened to Master Silandra. They were partners as Master and Padawan and worked together. Rooper didn't remember what it had been like to have a mother or father guiding her instead of Silandra. Someone who might not share her beliefs and priorities but whom she still loved.

Sky said, "The San Tekkas already had an agreement with Spence to sponsor him in the race, and I didn't think he'd switch to a Graf ship just because I asked."

"Grafs have a . . ." Dass winced.

Sky grinned at Dass. "A less sparkling reputation than the San Tekkas. So I offered to sponsor Dass directly."

Rooper glanced between them, but her gaze settled on Dass. "Dass, your father is going to be so worried."

The young prospector took Rooper's hands. "Not if you're with us. He trusts you—he knows Jedi won't let me be hurt."

"That's oversimplifying. . . ." Rooper squeezed his hands back.

"It would really help us out to have a Jedi on our team, too. Not just to keep us safe," Sky said, clearly indicating they didn't think they needed Rooper's protection. They needed her for something else.

Rooper studied Sky for a moment. There was something she was missing still, that they hadn't told her, but in a flash of clarity, Rooper realized she wanted to be convinced. She wanted to go with Dass and Sky. Whether that was her own frustrations with the lack of communication from Jedha, feeling stuck, or an awareness gifted to her by will of the Force, Rooper wasn't sure yet.

"I'm listening," she said, talking both to Dass and to the Force.

Sky Graf *loved* the *Brightbird*.

Sky's older brother, Helis, had commissioned the ship offworld, but two years earlier, when Sky was thirteen, he'd brought it to Thelj to finalize the programming, add some decorative touches (like the tiny white lights strung across the ceiling of the cockpit for whimsy, and actual ice-swan-down pillows in the crew quarters for comfort), and of course load the family Graffian codes, which had to be done by hand. At first Helis would only let Sky help with the ship's decor, but recently Sky had been overseeing all work on the ship while Helis was off on Travyx

Prime flirting with a San Tekka, of all people, and organizing the hyperspace race. Sky couldn't believe Helis risked so much spending all that time with a San Tekka—their families were ultimate rivals! They'd never be allowed to see each other socially. (Sky refused to consider that the taboo was exactly what their brother liked about Precoria San Tekka.)

But the *Brightbird* itself was perfect. And Sky supposed they had Precoria to thank for distracting Helis enough for Sky to borrow the starship. It had been easy, really. The *Brightbird* was a Graf starship, which meant Sky knew its ins and outs. It was not stealing. Sky had tried to convince Helis to let them track down Planet X. They'd argued their heart out and offered to work together, but Helis was stubborn as a Gamorrean and not good at sharing. Sky had had no choice but to take the *Brightbird*. Helis could always team up with his girlfriend Precoria if he still wanted to be in the race.

Now a Jedi Padawan was aboard, and honestly, Sky couldn't be more excited. But they'd play it cool. No need to alert this very baby Jedi that Sky had been hearing stories about Jedi their whole life and even went through an embarrassing phase when they were about seven where they painted an air-recycler tube bright blue and pretended it was a lightsaber. Worse was the time Sky had rigged up a series of magnets and magnetized plasma dust in the Thelj compound's family room to make it look like they could send a handful of stress balls across the space in an elaborate dance using the Force alone.

It had been impressive! And fun. Dad had loved it. Mom and Aunt Jacinda were major fun-killers and told Sky to apply themself harder to probability theory and developing their own dialect in Graffian code. Sky had been born with the distinctive privilege of being a Graf, Aunt Jacinda liked to say, and it was their duty to make themself worthy of the name and resources. But Dad had laughed so hard at Sky's Force trick that his cheeks pinked, and he hugged Sky onto his lap. Dad was the one who'd told Sky the Jedi stories—he was from Coruscant, and supposedly one of his great-aunts or someone had been a Jedi. Sky had hoped, maybe, it was possible some Force sensitivity would suddenly blossom in them, until Dad—

Well. It had been over a year since Sky had heard anything from their dad.

Sky pushed aside that line of thinking and focused on convincing the cute Jedi to join them.

Dass Leffbruk had hold of the Padawan's hands, smiling excitedly. Sky liked Dass a lot—he was sharp and enthusiastic and really looked up to his dad, despite the fact that he was, well, ditching him. Sky looked up to their dad, too, and at first couldn't imagine doing what Dass was doing. But it was different: Dass needed to be his own person, and this was the best way for him to prove himself. For Sky, this trip was about the same thing—only it wasn't their dad they needed to prove themself to. It was the entire Graf clan.

The Padawan, Rooper, stared at Dass for a moment, then swung her bright eyes to Sky. Sky felt pinned in place: not afraid but kind of overwhelmed. Rooper said, "I'm listening."

"We're going to get to Planet X," Dass said.

Rooper didn't look away from Sky. "You think you can get Dass to the planet faster than his dad or Sunshine Dobbs or any other experienced prospectors?"

"It helps that most other prospectors won't really be looking for something they don't think exists," Dass admitted.

"Sure do." Sky answered Rooper confidently, as if Dass hadn't spoken. They were excellent at pretending to be confident. Confidence was prized by Grafs, and Sky knew how to fake it. Just like they understood when to push and when to let others do the talking.

Act confident, be confident, Aunt Jacinda always said.

Know yourself, and you'll find your own confidence, Dad would say quietly instead.

Rooper tilted her head. Her black hair was tied in a braid, but a few strands fell to her shoulder at the motion. She was petite, with a cute nose on a pretty brown face, but something about her radiated competence. Maybe it was the lightsaber at either hip, or the brown robes, or the way she held herself. Sky kind of hoped all Jedi seemed that way, though. Their eyes went to the little Padawan braid against Rooper's neck. Excitement bubbled in their stomach.

Sky wanted to confess immediately that they'd always wanted to meet a Jedi, but that probably wasn't the best way to start. "You've already noticed, I'm sure, what a beauty the *Brightbird* is."

"Yes, this ship is definitely much nicer than any prospecting ship I've ever seen before."

Dass snorted a laugh, and Sky asked, "You know how prospecting works, usually?"

"The basics," Rooper said, then sipped her probably tepid tea.

Dass took over eagerly. "For regular prospecting we use old-fashioned star maps to make very short jumps that we're pretty certain have no occlusions—something that interrupts hyperspace. An obstacle, like the gravity around a planet or an asteroid field. As we make the little jumps, we leave beacons behind like bread crumbs. If we get to an obstacle, we go around it, marking the way. When we find an end point, like an inhabited planet or a moon, then we link the beacons and register the route from where we started to where we ended. Then we can sell the route to somebody who will lay out more sophisticated beacons, and there you have an official hyperspace lane."

Sky noticed Rooper purse her lips in distaste, and interrupted: "This is how the Republic gets their routes, too. They buy from prospectors—or hire their own."

Rooper nodded. "So why is it so hard to find Planet X?"

"Nobody even really knows the direction to start jumping," Sky said.

"Right." Dass straightened his shoulders. "And there's something around the planet that . . . just kind of resists mapping. Anybody who actually mapped a safe route to Planet X would be rich. Most routes are more mundane, but just as important for expanding the frontier. Teams in the Hyperspace Chase are encouraged, but not required, to accept sponsorship from Graf or San Tekka. With sponsorship you get trademarked, specially developed hyperspace beacons. There's also a wide-ranging agreement that prospectors with the Graf or San Tekka beacon codes will be left alone for the time of the Chase."

"Left alone?" Rooper frowned.

"You know," Dass said, "by pirates, smugglers. Hutts. Also . . . there've been more aggressive planetary navies given that war between Eiram and E'ronoh."

Rooper looked down at her empty teacup.

Sky reached to pour more.

Dass said, "I need to get back to that planet for my ship. The only holo of my mom is still there. And my dad needs it, too, needs me to do this for him because he won't. I can, though. *We* can. You'd be helping me, Rooper."

Even Sky, who'd just met the Padawan, saw that hit home. Rooper met Dass's hopeful, eager gaze. She touched one of her hands over her heart.

Sky leaned closer. Now was the moment to clinch the deal. "We need you."

"Why? Why do you need a Jedi, Sky Graf?"

Sky took a deep breath. "Because I have a . . . compass. Well, it's not really a compass, more like a resonator. But it can help us navigate through hyperspace, in the direction of Planet X. Without beacons."

"That's impossible!" Rooper said. "Without beacons, you've got nothing for the navicomputer to lock on to for making the calculations. You could run into a rogue asteroid field or an electromag storm, or anything, really! Anomalies!"

Sky held out their hand. "Listen, that's why I was talking about the basics of prospecting before. This thing is ancient tech. My dad excavated it, and we don't entirely understand it. But it does work! It's got supraluminite, just like a lot of compasses, and if you have something from the place you want to go, a stone or seeds, the supraluminite in this device resonates with it, and it's like it remembers where that thing came from. Then it points the way."

"What do you have from Planet X?" Rooper asked, in a tone that suggested she didn't really want to know.

Dass smiled eagerly at her. "We have *me*."

Sky laughed at Rooper's shocked expression. They really liked Dass. He was hard to predict, Sky had found. Nervous sometimes, bold other times. But when he wanted something, he held on to it.

Rooper said, "That's dangerous. And it sounds impossible. How can supraluminite trace an object—especially a person—back to its place of origin through resonance?"

"I think you can help with that," Sky said. "Doesn't the Force connect everything in the galaxy?"

"Yes, but not . . ." The Padawan looked past Sky for a moment as though trying to see the right words to explain. "Not with specific frequencies that can be . . . tapped into or calculated. If that was the case, I would be able to work like your device and trace the Force from one place to the next. But I can't. No Jedi can do that. We'd definitely have that recorded."

"Just because it's never been proven doesn't mean it isn't possible," Dass said urgently.

"That's just not how the Force works." Rooper glanced at Dass. "I'm sorry, Dass, but there's no way this is true."

Dass drooped, but Sky shook their head. "Rooper, aren't

you willing to at least try? What if you're wrong? It could be a huge discovery. Not just to find Planet X, but it could revolutionize how you understand the Force! What's the point of not even trying?"

Rooper met Sky's gaze again, and for a long moment Sky felt like maybe they could feel Rooper listening to her instincts—and to the Force. Finally the Padawan said, "I shouldn't agree to this, no matter what. It's too dangerous. We're not equipped for it."

"We are," Sky said, offended on behalf of their ship.

"Master Silandra expects me to be on Batuu."

"Didn't you say she's on Jedha?" Dass said. Sky winced. They didn't know much, but they'd heard something bad had happened on that moon only days earlier.

Rooper's gaze shot to Sky. "How good are your comms?"

"Oh, they're excellent." Sky smiled their best smile. "Especially off-planet. Our relay is incredible thanks to the *Brightbird*'s design. The ship itself might as well be a triple-powered comms buoy! We might be able to reach directly to Jedha. Especially once we start jumping."

Rooper bit her lip.

Sky tried to be patient. This had already taken too

long, and the *Brightbird* needed to get off Batuu before Helis caught up to them. He had to be close behind Sky—and even sent his goons ahead to try to get the ship back. Sky could hold off hired mercenaries, but they didn't think they could keep Helis from getting into the ship he knew at least as well as Sky did.

They decided to press a little bit harder. "The Hyperspace Chase lasts two weeks," Sky said. "Let's make a deal. You go with us for those two weeks. Help us, do your Jedi thing, and at the end, whether we find Planet X or not, the *Brightbird* will take you anywhere you want to go."

"And," Dass said, "you can use the comms as much as you want while we're traveling, to find out where Master Silandra is."

Rooper looked between Dass and Sky. Sky smiled their friendliest, brightest smile, trying to appear totally calm and innocent.

"Okay," Rooper said.

Dass whooped and threw his arms around her.

Fel Ix withdrew the datacard with the specialized code from the comms buoy. They'd harnessed the buoy about an hour earlier and dragged it into the small cargo hold of their stealth shuttle. Since then, he and Chal, a gray Ardennian with a cold temper and four arms—along with a red astromech—had been surgically removing a few key components and replacing them with the Graffian codes he'd memorized. Fel Ix had never worked this way before, with a long-distance slicer shortcut. But with these special codes, he could take any comms buoy and turn it into a private one that could be controlled only by the Path.

Now it was time to wipe the buoy's memory and release it back to its post in the middle of nowhere.

The astromech beeped, and Fel Ix handed over the card data. "That should do it," he said softly to Chal.

Chal hummed acknowledgment. Their long fingers curled into fists, and their second pair of arms stretched behind their back to hit a few buttons on the hold control panel.

This was the second buoy they had altered. They had a map of exactly which buoys would be most effective in bringing frontier-wide communication to a crashing stop if the Mother chose to activate the kill switch they were installing with the slicer code. It was supposed to give her the ability to not only kill the whole network but bring down comms in targeted systems, too. The focus was around Dalna, where the Path of the Open Hand had lived for so long before taking to the stars on the *Gaze Electric*. Fel Ix did not know what the Mother had planned, but he trusted her visions from the Force. She had already used the buoys to spread her message about Jedha as far as it could reach. The Mother had expressed her dismay and sorrow at the tragedy of the battle and promised aid to the Convocation of the Force to make up for it. But to Fel Ix's shock, the Mother had also said that the Herald was behind the attack. The Herald had been a leader of the Path alongside the Mother, and Fel Ix had trusted him. It was difficult to believe he would betray them, but if the Mother said so, that must be the truth.

Before Fel Ix and Chal could initiate the release of the buoy, the ship's comm crackled and their third crew member, a human named Severn, said, "Fel Ix, a Republic ship just jumped into range. They're calling us."

"Respond with the Republic code. I'll be right there," Fel Ix said. He was younger than Chal and Severn, but the Mother had put him in charge. So he had to be the one to talk to the Republic.

Fel Ix did not wipe his hands on the legs of his jumpsuit. He was not excreting stress oils. He wasn't that nervous.

It was a quick jog to the cockpit from the cargo hold. Severn waited, standing at the comms station. She looked relieved to see Fel Ix. Fel Ix moved to take over and tapped a few buttons to magnify the Republic ship on the viewport. It was small—not the kind that would be heavily armed, and unlikely to be carrying Jedi. Fel Ix gave his hopes to the will of the Force and pressed the comm. "This is the *Way of Clarity*. Can we help you?"

"Code acknowledged, *Way of Clarity*. This is the *Felicitations*. We weren't aware of any Republic comms teams in the area."

"We aren't a Republic comms team, *Felicitations*. We were dispatched from a substation in the Ileenium system after a report from a passing cargo vessel that this buoy was acting up. We have it in for diagnostics but will release shortly."

"Roger, *Way of Clarity*. Will wait for buoy signal."

Fel Ix's cheek furls twitched in frustration, but he didn't let it into his voice. "Fine. Just a few moments."

Fel Ix turned off the ship-to-ship comm and glanced at Severn. "Keep monitoring them as best you can without letting on, and make sure everything is prepped to jump to hyperspace."

Then Fel Ix rushed back to the cargo hold, where Chal and the astromech had loaded the comms buoy—all two meters of it—into the airlock for redeployment. Fel Ix helped adjust the small radio antenna while Chal activated the buoy, and then they both stepped back to start the process of opening up the ship.

Instead of watching, Fel Ix returned to the cockpit. He got notification from the hold that the release was successful, and he watched the little buoy, which was half droid, half giant antenna, turn on its thrusters to regain its assigned location in the comms network.

Surreptitiously, Fel Ix had Severn flick on the slicer code, and they listened as the Republic ship *Felicitations* tested the buoy.

Of course it worked just fine. The other ship sent acknowledgment and farewell, then continued on its way.

Fel Ix sank into the chair at the nav station.

Chal appeared in the cockpit, bottles of water in three of their four hands. "That was close," they said in a totally flat tone. They offered water to Fel Ix and Severn.

Before Fel Ix could reply, a tiny green light appeared on the comms station.

"It's coming through the buoy on the Mother's channel," Severn breathed.

Fel Ix handed the water back to Char and told Severn, "Respond with our code."

A string of beeps and hissing noises crackled from the comms station, then the deep, soothing voice of the Mother herself: "Fel Ix. If your mission is proceeding well, you will easily receive this message. Continue as planned, but keep on the lookout for any Jedi and report their presence back to me immediately. They will be coming toward Dalna in greater numbers, and they are a threat to the safety of our family. We must protect the Force."

Then the Mother's voice cut out. It felt like Fel Ix couldn't breathe for a moment. He turned his hands over, palms up, and took a deep breath. "Severn, send back this message: 'The Force will be free.'"

CHAPTER
SEVEN

For the first time in his life, Dass Leffbruk hit the switch to drop a ship out of hyperspace, from the pilot's chair. And not just any pilot's chair—one on a Graf ship, with all the up-to-date tech and fancy gadgets. He let himself imagine owning, or at least leasing, a ship like this someday. Smooth and carefree in its transitions, with shiny and sleek switches and excellent snacks. It was so much better than the *Silverstreak*. Dass felt bad thinking so, but it was true. His dad's ship was held together with flex-tape and hope. This one had components so new he hadn't even heard of them. Maybe if they'd had a ship like this, his mom wouldn't have died.

With a little jolt, the *Brightbird* emerged from hyperspace at the edge of the Travyx system, just a short flight from Travyx Prime. Dass carefully caressed the controls before settling his hands at the ready.

Sky said this system had been chosen for the start of this year's Hyperspace Chase because it had a highly developed populace and served as one of the strongest agrarian hubs in the frontier. There were rumors that the Republic would be opening an official hyperspace lane directly from the Core Worlds out to the frontier sometime soon and that Travyx might be in the running. That meant more traffic, more credits, and plenty of opportunity for both the Grafs and San Tekkas to open a variety of private lanes for future trade and luxury routes.

The *Brightbird* was scheduled to enter the gravity well of Travyx Prime with the rest of the prospecting teams. From there they'd send their registration code. Then would come the only tricky part of the flight: lining up with the rest of the contestants at the edge of the planet's gravity to wait for the starting signal. Sky had promised Dass could take them on their first short hyperspace jump, too.

Dass was only twelve and had already seen so much: the basalt forests of Perlandia and the grass seas of Tiikae, the last gasps of a blue sun, brilliant rainbow anomalies near the belt of Urn-Aram, the weird blobs of energy like bubbles of water hanging in space that surrounded Planet X—and the mystery planet itself.

But this was the first time he'd piloted a ship. And for it to be such a shiny, pretty thing as the *Brightbird* made Dass want to do a little tap dance.

He did wish his dad were there, but then, if he were, Dass wouldn't be flying at all. He'd maybe be allowed to run the comms station. Maybe. Since Gloam—and Sunshine betraying them—Spence had gotten even more protective of Dass, which Dass understood. They'd almost died! But he hated it. Dass had lived his whole life exploring the frontier, and he wanted to keep doing it. That was another reason he'd been glad to set out with Sky instead of his dad. He could do it! He just needed the chance. If they succeeded in their mission, not only would Dass be famous in prospecting circles for finding the route to Planet X, he'd probably catch the eye of the Republic and be able to easily join a Pathfinder team when he was old enough.

Pathfinder teams explored the frontier on behalf of the Republic, with a pilot and medic and comms team, and usually a Jedi and Padawan. When Dass thought about it, he, Sky, and Rooper were like their own unofficial Pathfinder team. He'd have to tell Rooper that. She might find it inspiring, too.

As he angled the *Brightbird* toward Travyx Prime, the planet gleamed in the light of its sun. Its five moons clustered in a tight orbit near one of the poles, and arcing around the planet like a ring of ice and gas was the Hyperspace Chase starting line.

"Wow," Dass murmured.

Leaning over him, Sky laughed. "Yeah."

Rooper stepped up to join them, also gazing out the viewport.

Ship after ship came into focus: big cargo transports with rows of long-range comms satellites, little short-range shuttles fitted out with bulbous hyperspace engines, sleeker vessels with heavy durasteel noses, and plenty of the more haphazard-looking prospecting ships Dass was used to.

The starting line was marked by bright blue beacons that flashed slowly. Sky turned toward the comms, but hesitated.

Rooper said suspiciously, "What's wrong?"

"Nothing!" Sky said, and hit the button to send their code.

But Rooper wasn't buying it. As Dass paid attention to maneuvering the ship, he saw Rooper in his peripheral vision put her hands on her hips. "You did steal this ship."

"I did . . . not." Sky spread their hands. "I helped build it. My brother registered it."

"I can tell you're not being honest, Sky," Rooper chided.

Sky dug their fingers into their furrowed stripes of black-and-white hair. "I wasn't supposed to take it. Helis was going to pilot it in the Chase. But it's not *stolen*."

With a soft sigh, Rooper nudged Sky out of the way and sat at the comms station. "I'm sending my message now."

"Wait for the return codes," Sky said. "We need them to reset the beacons I have on board in order to count in the race."

It took only another second before the Chase organizers sent back confirmation codes. From the comms station, Rooper routed them to Sky with a little pout. Sky loaded them into a datapad and rejoined Dass at the front of the cockpit. Rooper swiftly contacted the Travyx station and confirmed they could relay a message all the way to Jedha. Then she uploaded a different message for the nearest Republic Office of the Frontier, since that was how she'd contact Master Silandra the fastest. Before they'd departed Batuu, Rooper had sent a message to the Jedi outpost to explain her sudden disappearance and a similar message to the Republic office—one for the Jedi Master assigned to the outpost and one for Silandra in case she arrived back on Batuu. Finally, and this was the part Dass dreaded, Rooper pinged the Travyx subspace relay station again and asked after the prospecting ship the *Algo's Progress*.

That was the San Tekka ship his dad was on. Or should be. Dass *had* left a note for Spence explaining that he wasn't going with him to the race and not to worry, that Dass would be with Rooper. It wasn't even a lie! And Dass thought his dad had probably been relieved not to have Dass on the *Algo's Progress*, because it would be dangerous. Spence would definitely be more likely to successfully map out strong hyperspace lanes if he wasn't worried about his son.

"Forward thrusters," Sky murmured. "Spin a little to face point oh-three-two. . . . That's . . . that's right."

Listening to Sky, Dass turned them into place at the end of the starting lineup. He had to correct slightly, but he was getting the feel of the controls.

Just as Sky clapped a hand on his shoulder, the comms station beeped and Rooper flicked it on. "This is *Brightbird*," she said.

"Rooper Nitani!" came Spence Leffbruk's voice through a crackle. "Is that really you?"

"Yes, Mr. Leffbruk."

"What are you doing out here? I didn't think Jedi were involved in this."

"We're not. But I have someone with me who needs to tell you something."

Dass's stomach clenched. He did not want to do this. Better for his dad to think he was safe on Batuu. But Rooper had made it part of her bargain.

"Oh?" Spence said. "Is it Rok? I was meaning to get back to—"

Rooper glared at Dass and whispered severely, "Dass!"

"Uh, hi, Dad!" Dass yelled toward the comms.

Silence stretched from the other ship.

Then . . . "Dass! What in the seven moons— *Are you on that ship?*"

Dass let Sky nudge him out of the pilot's chair to take over while Dass moved nearer the comms. "I'm fine, Dad. I'm with friends—and Rooper. You know she'll—"

"This is not a place for kids! Are you all—"

Suddenly, the ship-to-ship comms cut out.

Rooper gasped, but Sky said, "Oops! That's enough of that." They'd cut it off from the pilot station.

"Sky," Rooper began.

"Listen, he fulfilled his part of the deal. His dad knows where he is! And we managed to get here right before the starting time, and we only have a minute," Sky said. "Can you run scans? I want to know if any other ships are paying attention to us."

"Because you stole this ship from your brother."

Sky rolled their eyes. "Dass—"

"Wait," Rooper said, still fixated on the comms system. "I want to search for any reports on the holonet about what happened on Jedha, and—"

"Like I was saying," Sky said over Rooper, "Dass, fire up the navicomputer. Take us anywhere you want, but quick. We need to get away from the other teams as fast as possible."

"Why?" Rooper jerked her attention to Sky.

"Well . . . the start of the Chase can be a bit"—Sky grimaced—"violent."

Rooper's brown eyes widened. "Sky! What have you gotten us—"

"Attention, prospectors!" A voice filled the cockpit as the Travyx authorities overrode all other signals. "This is Precoria San Tekka on the *Purrgil's Dream*, happy to welcome you to the seventh official Hyperspace Chase! You all have your codes and should have collected your beacons.

As you all know, the rules are simple: set your coded beacons at each point on your routes, and use your official registration to log the time and date of any completed lanes in order for them to qualify immediately. Other than that, have fun, and make my family some money! In just a few moments, we'll let the race begin!"

Sky said, "As soon as the mark hits, I'll pull us starboard and out of the planet's gravity as fast as possible. You just have the first jump ready, Dass!"

"We didn't collect any beacons," Dass said. "How will we mark the route we find?"

"There are beacons already on board, and I have the right codes now that we got the official prize code addendum," Sky said as if it should be obvious.

"The *Algo's Progress* just broke formation," Rooper said.

Sky snorted. "You're the one who made Dass's dad go and worry!"

"We're being contacted by the *Purrgil's Dream*, too."

Sky grimaced so big it showed all their teeth. "That's Precoria's ship. She knows my brother, she knows the ship. Ignore it!"

Dass tried to ignore them, too, to focus on setting some coordinates. Guilt at leaving his dad also threatened to distract him. But Dass knew he was making the right choice. He had to get back to Planet X and to whatever was left of the *Silverstreak*, and his dad had refused again and again. Working with Sky Graf was his only option. And Sky had told him when they first reached out that they could trust each other because they wanted the same thing: to find Planet X and prove themselves. Besides, Sky was just so clever and charming.

Dass reined in his worries and got to focusing. For this first short jump, Dass didn't want to take the *Brightbird* too far; they could jump right back the way they'd come and start from there with the resonator device. Yes, that was a good idea. Probably none of the others would do that. . . .

"Ready! Set!" Precoria San Tekka cried through the radio. "And . . ."

The viewport lit up with vivid explosions of blue, white, and yellow in a long arcing line.

"Go!" Sky cried as they threw forward the thruster lever and the *Brightbird* lurched into the race.

CHAPTER EIGHT

Seconds after they darted forward, the ship beside them burned faster ahead, turned, and shot a long stream of clouds across their nose.

Sky cursed and leaned back as they pulled the *Brightbird*'s nose up and flipped them over to curl away. The pink gas rolled over the viewport, and they burst through it into the star field again.

"What are they doing?" demanded Rooper.

Dass called over his shoulder, "Diversion tactics! This is the only time we'll all be together, so everyone wants a head start."

"Are those . . ." Sky said wonderingly.

Rooper peered out the viewport as another ship in the distance dropped what looked like big silver eggs behind it.

"Mines!" Sky finished their thought.

Shocked, Rooper watched as the eggs exploded in little fiery pops. She reached out with the Force but also made sure her acceleration straps were secure.

"Ready with those jump coordinates, Dass?" Sky asked, their voice higher than usual as they banked left, then shot the nose vertical and kept going. "We'll be clear to jump in one minute."

"I can't believe they're dropping mines!" cried Rooper.

"Ion mines! They'll knock us out, not kill us," Sky called.

"Yep!" Dass said, answering Sky's question. "One minute ahead, then come around to point three-six!"

Rooper reached over and grabbed one of Dass's acceleration straps, too, tugging it until the boy got the idea and fastened it. He shot her a grin.

"I never expected to be in a ship dodging mines," Rooper said to herself.

"Welcome to the frontier," Sky tossed over their shoulder.

"Prospectors like to win," Dass added.

"Not make friends," Rooper said. She managed not to squeeze her eyes closed and was glad for the *Brightbird*'s compensators that kept her body from feeling their extreme velocity. Mostly.

"I'm glad we're friends," Dass said. His eyes were big and round, making him look a little panicked, a little thrilled. He gave her a very goofy grin.

Rooper started to smile back. Just then Sky cursed and jerked at the helm. The ship lurched up and away.

Outside the viewport bright pink and red lights exploded.

"Flares!" Sky called. "Just light!"

The light brightened as Sky flew the *Brightbird* directly through it. Rooper clenched her jaw against a scream.

They blasted through the pink-red flares, and Rooper blinked quickly.

Sky leaned toward the viewport, one hand dancing over the controls while the other held the helm.

"Is that . . ." Dass started to ask, pointing out into space.

It looked like a ship had turned midflight and was aiming right for the nose of another ship.

"Not our problem," Sky said.

Rooper's mouth dropped open. "Can't you do something?"

"They're just playing chicken, distracting each other."

The *Brightbird* trembled. It sounded suddenly like somebody had thrown a thousand pebbles against the cockpit shielding. "Argh!" Sky cried. "Comm-poppers! Rooper, are they jamming anything?"

Rooper's pulse raced. She keyed into the comms, and a few of the channels were blank, but not all of them. "We're all right for now, but I—" Feedback from the channel she was on screeched through the cockpit. She clapped her hands over her ears.

"Hit that yellow button—the flashing one!"

Rooper slammed her hand down, and the noise cut out. But Rooper didn't have time to slump in relief. Prospectors were a menace!

Outside the ship, another prospector shuttle blazed past, and in its wake more flares burst to life. They formed a huge shape. . . . It was . . . Rooper peered out the viewport, shocked and appalled. The flares formed the shape of a silver-white Wookiee, with some kind of paint turning its long fur into rainbows. The Wookiee snarled. Rooper was definitely distracted.

Sky laughed loudly. "Dass, nearly there?"

"Almost . . . almost . . ."

Just then the comms lit up, dragging Rooper's attention back to the moment. A young, angry voice blared through the cockpit. "Sky Graf, stop right this minute—"

"No, thanks!" Sky cried, cutting the comms off again.

"Who was that?" Rooper demanded.

"My brother, Helis! He finally caught up with—"

Suddenly, the lights on the comms station in front of Rooper flashed and then went dark, and Sky screeched in fury. "Helis sliced into the *Brightbird*!" they hissed, hands flying over the controls. The *Brightbird* lurched.

"Is that a tractor beam?" Rooper asked.

"No, he's slicing into the controls," Sky said. "Rooper, open that channel back up for me—Dass, hold on to those coordinates until I kick him out!"

Rooper struggled with the blinking comms, and Dass gritted his teeth and gave commands to the navicomputer.

"Helis, let us go. I'm in command of the ship. Let me go!" Sky yelled into the open channel. Then they turned the ship hard, only to be blocked by a blazing white ship—much too close for safety.

Somebody had decided to play chicken with them, after all!

Sky spun them, the whole ship tilting wildly, and tried to go under the other ship. "How did he even get here so fast?" they grumbled under their breath.

"I won't let up, Sky. That's my ship. This is my race," Helis Graf yelled through the garbled comms.

Rooper stared at the system, wishing she knew what to do to isolate them, or their frequency. "There's nothing I can do," Rooper said to Sky. "I don't know the system."

"How are you at flying, then?" Sky asked, peeling away from Helis's ship in a stomach-churning corkscrew.

Rooper shook her head. Master Silandra claimed she was more than qualified to pilot, but she didn't know the *Brightbird*!

"I can fly!" Dass said, unbuckling his belt. "Rooper, take over the nav!"

The three switched places fast, Sky turning the pilot seat to Dass, then slamming into the comms station. "Rooper, any short jump will do. Dass, keep us away from Helis!"

Sky was snarling at their brother and punching switches on the comms with one hand while they dug open a small panel under the station and started pulling out wires.

"I designed those codes, Sky," Helis said. "You can't lock me out without disabling your whole system."

"I have my own codes, you jerk," Sky muttered. Then Sky fell out of their chair as Dass banked high. "Can you two hurry up?" Sky cried, clambering to their knees. "I've stripped his signal back, but he'll—*argh!* No, Helis is back. . . ."

Rooper said, very strained, "Dass, I have a jump ready, in twenty seconds if you can get to this mark?"

It lit up on Dass's display. "Yes!" he crowed. "Ready, Sky?"

"Just . . . about . . ."

"Sky!" Helis yelled, and then he was cut off.

"Now!"

"Hold on!"

Rooper grabbed the arms of her chair and stared out the viewport as Dass spun them, yelled *mark*, and hit the hyperspace key. The ship leapt forward, and the stars blurred into a tunnel of light.

CHAPTER NINE

A relieved silence filled the cockpit. They were safe. In hyperspace. Nobody really knew what hyperspace was, exactly, other than a different plane of space. From outside it couldn't be changed or affected by people, only by objects and forces that affected all space. So nobody could hurt them as long as their coordinates and beacons were good.

"The jump is less than an hour," Dass said, sounding a little breathless.

Sky hit a few buttons, then stood. They stretched, and the armor on their jumpsuit creaked. "Whew. I think we should familiarize you two with the resonator device so that when we get to our stop, we can fire it up and move on."

Dass nodded eagerly. "Where is it?"

"In my bunk," Sky said. "I'll get it."

"I'll make a snack," Dass said, and rushed off. But Rooper hung back with Sky. She walked with them down the corridor to Sky's narrow quarters at the rear of the ship. Inside was plain, not decorated—which made sense, Rooper thought, if Sky borrowed the ship without permission. There was only a single holobook on the slide-out desktop beside the bunk, and rumpled blankets.

Sitting on the floor was a large disk of what looked like copper, with a shimmering inlay around the edge and in the center. Delicate astromeridian lines were etched onto the surface, and a small chunk of pale pink stone rested in the concave middle. It seemed to be nothing but decorative. Rooper crouched and placed a hand lightly on the metal edge. It felt like regular metal. She drew a long breath, reaching out for the Force. It brightened with warm colors, like a living being might. The Force flowed through it, without shadows or anything that might be a warning. Just like the Force flowed through everything.

"Help me lift it?" Sky asked.

But Rooper stood instead, quickly facing Sky. "Wait," she said. She leaned close to the other teen, near enough to see the gray around their pupils. Rooper hadn't had any time alone with Sky since this entire disaster mission began. "First, I want to know why you're really so interested in Planet X."

"Obviously," Sky scoffed. "I already told you."

Rooper shook her head. "Not everything."

"Are you going to tell me everything?" Sky deflected.

"About what?"

"What you want."

Rooper sensed Sky was pushing her away because underneath their bravado Sky was in pain. So Rooper said, "I want to serve the Force. Help bring light to the galaxy, especially out here. I want to be strong, and good. Helpful. I want to make friends, and—I want my master to be proud of me." Rooper bit her lip. She thought of Silandra's inevitable reaction to Rooper's wildly agreeing to go on this adventure alone. But Silandra wasn't there, and Rooper didn't even know if Silandra had survived whatever happened on Jedha.

No—she'd know if Silandra had died. Silandra would

have become one with the Force, and Rooper would have felt that.

Rooper took another breath and held Sky's gaze. The other teen was watching her carefully. Rooper decided to be brutally honest. "I want to be successful here, with you and Dass, to help Dass. But I want to be right that it's the will of the Force for me to be here. For us to find Planet X. I'll get in less trouble that way."

That surprised Sky enough they snorted with laughter.

Rooper waited.

Slowly, Sky's guarded expression softened. "I want to find the planet because I want my family to be proud of me, too. But I have to prove to them I'm good enough. I'm smart, but that's not enough for the Grafs. We have to expand the Graf name and our reach in the frontier, like making new allies—creating beneficial connections with new worlds. Find ways to make fresh credits. Gamble well and win. Build the family fortune and reputation. The faster and younger we make our name, the better."

Rooper nodded. There was more, she could tell.

Sky rolled their eyes dramatically. "Glory! I'm doing it for the glory, and I guess that isn't something they let Jedi admit."

"Jedi aren't ambitious," Rooper agreed.

Sky laughed again. "Sure."

"We aren't . . . or at least, not about personal ambition," Rooper argued. "What we're doing out here isn't for the sake of the Jedi, or for power. It's just the will of the Force. To . . . make the galaxy brighter. For light."

It sounded naive even to Rooper, but that didn't make it less true. She thought again of Master Silandra and her preferred weapon: a shield. Silandra was a protector, not an aggressor. A lightsaber could be used to attack or defend; it was flexible and adaptable. But the shield was always a shield. A shield was devoted to being itself, Rooper thought, and blinked at her own realization.

Sky was looking at her with a quiet smile and a little bit of amusement. "Let's get this thing to the cockpit, yeah?"

Rooper bent to pick it up herself, refusing to be embarrassed. The device was about the size of a dinner plate and heavy, but she could manage it, especially with a little boost from the Force. She told herself she was not showing off for Sky.

Leading the way back down the shiny corridors to the

cockpit, Sky said, "You know, I've always thought Jedi were exciting."

"Oh," Rooper said. Now maybe she was a little embarrassed.

"My dad used to tell me stories about them. You. Appearing around the galaxy to right wrongs, fighting smugglers, that kind of thing. Also, he saw the Jedi Temple on Coruscant once. He said it glowed in the sun and the main tower has, like, a crown on top."

Rooper nodded and drew on the Force more so the resonator floated over her hands. She focused and pushed it ahead just a little bit.

"Wow," Sky said.

"It's good for my focus," Rooper said truthfully. This kind of concentrated control was one of the reasons Jedi sometimes trained by meditating while using the Force to float objects.

"I'm impressed."

"That's not—" Rooper turned to Sky, and the device wobbled slightly. She grimaced and returned her focus.

"Put it there by the navicomputer," Sky said as they stepped into the cockpit.

Dass was waiting with a little foldout tray covered in snacks. "Wow!" he said when he realized Rooper was using the Force to move the resonator device. "Is it funny that this is kind of more impressive than when you were fighting with your lightsabers on Gloam?"

Rooper was just starting to sweat down her spine when she placed the resonator delicately on the deck. "I think you were too distracted by the giant Katikoots to notice."

"Maybe," Dass said, eagerly plopping down next to the device.

Sky checked something on the control panel and then glanced back. "I'd like to hear that story," they said, and added hopefully, "and maybe see you demonstrate your lightsabers?"

It wasn't good to show off, Rooper reminded herself, but she had said she wanted to make friends, and the more people who liked Jedi out on the frontier, the better, right? Especially someone with the resources and curiosity of Sky Graf. Rooper nodded. "Maybe when one of our jumps is long enough, I can practice some forms."

Sky and Dass both grinned, and Sky clapped once. "Fantastic. Now let's see about getting this thing to work."

CHAPTER TEN

Dass's excitement grew as he listened to Sky explain the ancient device. It was something Sky's dad had uncovered during an excavation on Thelj more than five years earlier. The ice planet had once been temperate, before the sun imploded, and around the equator there were ruins buried under layers of glaciers that had preserved a lot very well. "Dad was the reason we built our compound on Thelj in the first place," Sky said proudly. "We're always looking for new ways to prospect and navigate. But Dad didn't think this thing belonged with that missing culture—it didn't match the style and composition of most of the ruins. He hypothesized that they'd been space-faring, too, and had found it elsewhere!"

"It's ancient," Dass said reverently. This was one of his favorite parts of prospecting: discovering lost things, seeing places people hadn't seen ever before—or at least not for a long time.

"Did your father know how to use it?" Rooper asked. Something about her soft voice made Dass wish his own dad were there. She sounded nostalgic for Sky's dad, and it made Dass feel the same about his. But if Spence were there, nobody would be speaking softly.

Sky didn't meet their eyes. "No. He had guesses, but I'm the one who figured it out after he was—gone."

Oh. Dass bit his lip and clenched his fists. His mom had died, too, and he didn't like talking about it. He missed her, though.

"I'm sorry," Rooper said.

"Don't be." Sky shrugged.

Dass reached over and poked Sky in the shoulder. Sky glared, but Dass just said, "So what did you figure out?"

Sky's expression cleared, and they pointed to the pinkish polished stone resting in the center of the device. It was large enough to fill the palm of Dass's hand and smooth. Sky said, "The supraluminite works like a lodestone, which is naturally magnetized, except this isn't attracted to metal or magnets. It matches resonances. It goes here, see?" Sky moved the lodestone to a slight indentation. "I discovered that it responded when I was just going through experiment after experiment with all kinds of possible triggers. Then I had this shaped to fit. There."

Nothing happened. Dass said, "I don't see anything."

"I feel it," Rooper murmured. "It's very . . . colorful. With the Force."

"It *is* a Force artifact?" Sky cried, and Dass couldn't tell if they were thrilled or appalled.

Rooper shook her head. "No, not . . . It wasn't made with the Force, or imbued with the Force the way artifacts are. But it"—she tilted her head as if listening to something Dass couldn't hear—"does resonate."

"I knew it. Will you monitor it?" Sky said. "Maybe you can tell if it's working." Rooper agreed, and Sky winked. "So convenient, having a Jedi around."

Dass leaned back, suddenly realizing that Sky was

flirting with Rooper. He blew out a big breath, puffing his cheeks. "Um, so, what do I do?" he said.

Rooper looked relieved.

"Welllll," Sky dragged out, "compasses usually have to be aligned with planetary magnetism somehow, or if it's for space, then aligned with something else. But this isn't aligned with anything like that."

"But like you said before, this doesn't seem to be an actual compass," Rooper said.

"Call it whatever you want," Sky said. "But it can match the resonance of another object and trace its location history."

Dass grinned. "How about the astro-resonance machine?"

"The *Graf* astro-resonance machine, if you insist." Sky laughed.

"Show me how it works," Rooper said, bringing them back to their purpose.

"All these etchings?" Sky pointed to the astromeridian lines. "Dad thought they mean the compass—*excuse me*, the resonance machine—can guide you through hyperspace. There's some more etchings from ruins in a language related to Old Jolynrian that agree, and they mention a stone and a key. The stone, I think, has to be the supraluminite, which initiates the machine and creates a field. Not just magnetic, but maybe of the Force, too? Connecting it to the resonance of the whole galaxy." Excitement slurred Sky's words together. They grasped Rooper's wrist.

"I told you I don't think that's possible. The Force isn't that simple. It isn't just resonance or a field or frequency. We talk about it"—Rooper shrugged—"a little metaphorically sometimes, but the Force isn't actually any of those things. People and places don't have . . . signatures in the Force." Rooper made a face.

"What?" Sky demanded.

"I can recognize how some people and places feel in the Force. But only if I know them well, if I . . . have learned their feeling. Their color." Rooper shook her head. "It isn't the same. You just have to believe me."

Sky turned their whole attention to Dass. "We're trying anyway. It worked on Thelj. When we're ready, Dass, we'll start with your finger—"

"Here," Dass said, reaching out to hover his finger over a small raised bed of copper beside the lodestone cradle. He was good with machinery, and even though this device was unlike anything he'd worked with before, Dass was pretty sure he understood the basic flow of the design. The only thing he wasn't seeing was a place for readouts. How were they going to receive the coordinates?

As if Sky had read his mind, they said, "Now we need to connect it to the navicomputer. I built a cradle to translate, and it's very amazing, if I do say so myself." Sky grinned. "Rooper, it's behind that storage panel next to the navicomputer."

Rooper popped open the panel and withdrew a tangle of metal fibers, relay lights, and connective ports. She raised her eyebrows in obvious skepticism. But Sky smiled. "It's to read the resonance machine's output for the navicomputer so the navicomputer can translate it into coordinates."

Just then, the navicomputer beeped. Dass leapt to his feet and flicked a switch. "We're coming out of hyperspace in five—four—three—two—one!"

The *Brightbird* slipped back into realspace with a gentle tremble.

Benign alerts lit up as the ship located itself, and Sky hunched over the pilot station. They were still a little breathless as they said, "Okay, we made it. Do you want to try this thing?"

"Yes!" Dass said instantly.

Rooper looked between the two of them. Dass nodded quickly, hoping she'd be ready. A slow smile bloomed on her face. "All right. And may the Force be with us."

CHAPTER
ELEVEN

Sky took a deep breath, ready to fly. This was the moment they'd been waiting for: using their discovery with the help of Dass to plot a course to Planet X—the same planet Dad had been obsessed with finding.

"This is dangerous," Rooper reminded them as she settled on the deck beside the resonance machine. "We don't know how this works."

"Space flight is always dangerous," Dass argued. "Especially prospecting. I'm ready!"

Sky knelt so they could reach both the astro-resonance machine and the nav station. Dass had pulled out some of the navicomputer's alloy wires, and together they looped the lattice cradle Sky had invented around the machine and stuck the correct input cable into the navicomputer port. The alloy wires looked like a tiny web—or like a map of hyperspace lanes. Sky pointed at it and said so to Dass.

"More like ice-spider webs than hyperspace, really," Dass said. He readjusted the goggles he wore like a headband to keep his curls out of his eyes.

"Poetic," Sky teased. They stared for another moment at the setup. Sky would be the first person to admit they didn't know exactly how this Graf astro-resonance machine worked. It was ancient tech, without an instruction manual. This was all Sky's guts and genius, plus Dass's courage and Rooper's certainty. They'd come too far to be deterred by mere ignorance! It would work or it wouldn't, and Dass could get them to Planet X either way. He had to.

Dass nodded and reached down to touch the ancient tech.

Rooper held his other hand. She closed her eyes. She'd taken off her golden-brown outer coat and sat on the cockpit floor in her layered robes and blue sash. Sky wasn't sure what she was doing, but then her entire energy just calmed. And the air around her seemed to follow suit, enough that Sky felt more balanced, too. Wow, they really liked having a Jedi around, even if she was just a Padawan. It was easy to imagine why most Grafs didn't want anything to do with "interfering Jedi," though.

Sky reached out and set the lodestone in place. Nothing happened.

"Think about Planet X," Sky said.

"I am." Dass's face wrinkled into a scowl of concentration.

They all just breathed. Sky found themself trying to match their breath to Rooper's. "It seems like it's not working," Dass said. He held his finger in place and looked all over the astro-resonance machine. "But . . ."

Rooper gasped. "Oh," she said.

"What?" Dass and Sky demanded simultaneously.

Biting her bottom lip a little, Rooper held her hand out. The supraluminite lodestone tilted, and instead of settling in the curve of the machine, it balanced on its edge.

Immediately, the lodestone began to glow very, very softly. Sky held their breath.

The pink lodestone continued its glow, and several of the astromeridian lines lit up, too.

Sky watched as the star map spun. It tilted, and different stars brightened and dimmed as the map swiveled.

"The colors are so bright," Rooper said.

"I feel it all humming," Dass said with a dopey grin. "It tickles my finger."

Sky thought they might tear up, they were so excited. It was working.

Suddenly, the proximity alert blared.

Sky spun, leaping to their feet to slam a hand on the button to activate the *Brightbird*'s shield array.

A shining white ship with long wings and a bulbous double nose appeared in the viewport. It had five black panels Sky suspected could be forward blaster ports. *Poodoo.* "Do you two have the coordinates yet?" they asked as the ship maneuvered quickly to put its double noses in the *Brightbird*'s path.

"Yes!" Dass cried. "The navicomputer is calculating now!"

"Is that your brother again?" Rooper said, standing behind Sky. One of her hands made a fist against her stomach. The other reached out over the resonance machine, holding the lodestone in place with the Force.

"Let's find out." Sky hit the pilot comms switch.

"Unknown vessel, this is the *Brightbird*. Get out of my way."

"This is the slightly inferior but still state-of-the-art *Starlily*, Sky. Lower your shields and prepare for docking." Definitely Helis. They could imagine his sneer perfectly, along with his coiffed black hair that never fell out of place and the purple rings pierced through his right ear that matched the rings in Sky's eyebrow.

"Sure, Helis, when the ice sharks arrange a tap dance," Sky said. They wished their brother was with them on this, but Helis hated sharing and didn't believe in what Sky and their dad believed in. He'd take the *Brightbird* and go flirt with his San Tekka girlfriend, wasting time mapping regular old hyperspace routes. Where was the glory in that?

"I will shoot, Sky," Helis threatened.

Dass said, "This is ready. We can jump if you get that ship out of our face."

"Okay . . ." Sky turned. "Rooper, you get ready in the cannon nest."

The Padawan lifted her eyebrows.

Sky pointed to the circular panel in the ceiling at the rear of the cockpit. Then they reached out and activated it on the control panel.

The white circle descended with a hiss.

"Sky!" Helis snarled through the comms. "Deactivate shields now."

"So you can infiltrate my comms again? I don't think so." To Rooper, Sky said, "That mini-lift will raise you into the nest. You'll fit easily."

Rooper spun and grasped the handles on the lift, stepping up into it.

"When you settle in, aim for their nose."

"I'm not firing on anybody," Rooper called over the hiss of the lift ascending again.

"Good!" Sky called back. "I don't want you to hurt my brother. Just disable the ship!"

"*Brightbird*, I will fire!" Helis yelled.

"Fine, Helis," Sky said into the comms. "Stand by. No need for violence."

Helis snorted.

The second the lift locked into place with Rooper above on the cannon, Sky dropped the shields and the *Brightbird*'s alarm sounded. Sky's pulse picked up.

"Sky . . ." Dass said slowly.

"I have a plan," Sky said to Dass and Rooper, who could

hear through the ship's comms. "Dass, be ready to hit the hyperspace activation. Rooper, are you ready with the targeting system?"

Rooper said, "It's still reading the ship—I think this system is *too* expensive for me to get a simple lock!"

Sky grimaced. Of course there was a downside to state of the art. "Use the Force!" they called up.

"That's not how the— Oh, never mind!"

Sky said, "Ready? Don't panic."

"What!" Rooper cried as Dass grabbed hold of the nav chair.

Sky hit a button and threw the thrusters forward. Their ship jerked directly toward the *Starlily.*

"Sky!" Rooper cried, and Dass made a little whine of surprise. Sky held firm.

Helis didn't want to hurt them—not Sky or the *Brightbird*; that would be Helis's priority. Maybe the *Brightbird* over Sky, after the stunt they'd pulled.

"Ready to jump?" Sky cried, leaning in, still aiming their ship at the other.

"R-ready!" Dass said.

"Fire, Rooper!"

"No!" Rooper yelled. "I won't risk lives for no good reason!"

"*Argh!*" Sky ground their teeth and pulled up just slightly, ready to skim the belly of the *Brightbird* against the upper nose of the other ship if they had to. But the other ship dropped—dropped and twisted, and just before Sky could yell at Dass to hit the jump lever, there was a flash of light and a concussion.

Sky fell as the *Brightbird* was jarred sideways. They landed hard on their hip and elbow, and their ears were ringing. They tried to tell Dass to go—go!

Blinking, Sky gritted their teeth and focused.

Dass slid into the pilot's chair, and mine-flares streaked across the viewport. Sky wanted to warn Dass that Helis probably had bigger mines to knock out their engine or comms, but it was too much effort.

The *Brightbird* twisted hard port and down, and then Dass's voice, which hadn't stopped, penetrated the ringing in Sky's ears. "—to hyperspace! Three . . . two . . . Oh, crap, wait . . . Two . . ."

The ship lurched, and Sky slammed their hands on the floor and dragged themself to the nav controls.

"One!" Dass yelled.

Sky grabbed the jump lever. They'd have to trust that Dass had piloted them out of any occlusions. They pulled.

Dass let out a long yell of glee and fear as the *Brightbird* rocketed into hyperspace.

Sky slumped down, leaning their forehead against the cool wall panel.

For a few minutes, they just breathed. Nearby, Dass did the same. The pilot's chair squeaked as he leaned to push something—a few somethings. Sky figured the kid had gotten them this far; they could just keep their eyes shut.

Then the lift from the cannon nest corkscrewed down with its signature puff of hydraulics.

But Sky was thinking about their dad. He'd have felt the same rush Sky was feeling. It had been such an awful year without him. Dad had taught them how to make educated guesses, how to confirm hypotheses, how to make up their own memory games to recall complex algorithms, how to tell if a plant needed watering, and the difference between being angry because they were hungry and angry because somebody was disrespecting them. Dad had gotten them their first chest binder when they were twelve, because they'd had a panic attack while getting dressed and managed to gasp out that there was something wrong with how they fit in Helis's old pilot vest, and if they couldn't fit in the vest, the simulator straps wouldn't lay right, and then they'd never learn how to pilot a speeder, much less a starship. And Dad had talked them through it, to find out what was actually bothering Sky. Dad said people made pilot vests and simulators for all kinds of bodies, so he thought there was something else going on, something about how Sky viewed their body compared with Helis, and asked why Sky thought they should fit perfectly into their brother's vest. Eventually, Dad helped Sky find the binder to ease their anxiety.

Sky's head ached with adrenaline, and their left ear still sang with a high-pitched ring. They wanted Dad. They hadn't had him in more than a year. Sky *needed* him. Nobody else ever listened like Dad. Understood like Dad.

Then gentle hands lifted them by the shoulders, and Rooper said, "Can you look at me, Sky? You hit your head."

Slowly Sky blinked. Rooper gazed into their eyes from very close, a pinch between her brows. In the pale light of the cockpit and shine of hyperspace out the viewport,

Rooper's cheeks gleamed a cool brown. She needed to rebraid her hair, Sky thought, and reached up to touch the little Padawan braid.

Rooper gently pushed Sky's hand away. "Please don't. I think you might have a concussion," she said softly, just as Dass thunked down on his knees beside them with the emergency med kit cradled against his chest.

"Yeah," Sky said, pushing up to sit a bit taller. They hadn't even realized they'd hit their head. "Thanks. Good—good flying, Dass."

Dass flushed immediately and fumbled opening the medpac.

Rooper touched Sky's chin and tilted up their head. "That was absolutely an insane plan. Flying right at them!"

Sky shrugged as Dass wiped antiseptic on their forehead. The wipe came away pinkish-red with blood. "My brother wants his ship mostly intact, at least."

Rooper snorted lightly. "Let's get you to your bunk and you can rest until we get out of hyperspace."

Sky let themself be guided but wasn't sure they remembered what being able to rest was really like.

CHAPTER
TWELVE

The first jump using coordinates from Sky's resonance machine took them to nothing. Rooper could tell Sky was trying to smile and be optimistic, but it seemed like maybe they were missing something. When they tried again, Rooper holding the supraluminite on its edge with the Force, Dass spoke aloud about Planet X and what he remembered from the chaotic landing and the smell of the air, and the machine seemed to work just like the first time. The *Brightbird*'s navicomputer crunched the information passed to it from the lattice Sky had engineered and offered up jump coordinates.

The focus on the Force helped Rooper remain calm. She was there in a support capacity, and it didn't matter to her very much if they found Planet X. It mattered to her friends, but it wasn't her goal. Hers was to keep them safe.

She thought about the small Jedi compass she'd brought with her from the archive. It would do no good in finding Planet X, but Rooper took it as a sign from the Force that she'd found it and brought it along. Rooper was supposed to be there. It was the will of the Force.

This jump lasted a few hours. Rooper convinced Sky to rest longer by agreeing to a lightsaber demonstration. She needed to meditate and practice anyway and told herself that having an audience was necessary because of the close quarters. It was *not* showing off.

They cleared the lounge floor, pushing the round table up against the galley and folding away all the little seats and the sofa bench. Then Rooper meditated while Sky and Dass made a meal.

It always felt strange to meditate in hyperspace. Rooper and her friends on the *Brightbird* existed in a small pocket of regular space, but their pocket hurtled through the different reality that was hyperspace. They traveled, but it didn't feel like they were moving. And maybe they weren't moving; maybe hyperspace curved around them, changing all the sense-making rules of time and light into a whirling mess. If Rooper thought about it too hard, she might get a headache.

So Rooper narrowed her focus. She could sense the *Brightbird* and both Dass and Sky, colorful with the living Force. And Rooper sensed herself, the blurry edges and spikes of her life, her energy, and her connection to the Force. She thought again about the epiphany she'd had about Master Silandra's shield: A shield was a shield. Meant to protect. Defend. It could be only what it was. She wanted to be devoted to being herself, too, especially this self that was so much a part of the Force.

Holding that balance in her heart, Rooper stood up and unsheathed her lightsabers. She moved into a series of forms with the sabers dormant. Then slowly she turned and thumbed on one saber, spun on the ball of her foot, then lit the other saber. The dual hum vibrated through her, like the Force itself flowed through her body, in her mind.

Rooper stepped through the forms she'd practiced as long as she could remember, careful, precise, and simple.

She kept going, then pushed even further, right to the edge of her abilities.

When she finished, she shut off both lightsabers at the same moment and held her pose.

She breathed hard. Sweat slid down her temples and spine and breastbone. She felt good.

Applause burst into the silence, and she blinked her eyes open at Dass and Sky, both of whom were clapping and grinning from their perch next to the galley.

Rooper licked her lips, then sheathed her lightsabers and wiped her forehead. Sky tossed her a lightweight towel.

Using it to mop at her neck, Rooper joined them. Dass pushed a fat-bottomed cup of water at her and said, "That was so great."

"It was," Sky added. "I'd love to get ahold of one of those weapons."

"You'd just pick it apart," Rooper found herself teasing.

Sky nodded, then winced.

"Head still hurt?" Rooper asked.

"Just a little. Food will help." Sky nudged at Dass, and they got up to serve the quick meal Dass had prepared: grass shark and spike herb soup he'd learned to make with his dad on Tiikae. Dass said he couldn't believe how many fresh ingredients from all over the frontier the galley contained. Sky shrugged with pride.

It was a nice few hours, relaxing with them. Rooper took a turn in the refresher to shower her sweat away and then took a nap. When she emerged, Sky and Dass had their arms elbow-deep in the guts of the entertainment system in the lounge, gently arguing about whether it saved energy to reroute some connector or another. Rooper was pretty sure whatever they were doing had shut down the entertainment system for a while, so she curled up on the sofa and listened. Tried not to worry about all the people missing her and Dass. Tried not to worry about what had happened on Jedha and to Master Silandra. Rooper had managed to catch a few lines of a holonet broadcast near Travyx before they'd had to run. There'd been a conflict of some kind, and a lot of chaos. The Jedi had been there, and several other members of the Convocation of the Force had been involved. There had been destruction in the city center, and one of the old Jedi statues had fallen in an explosion. There had been Jedi on Jedha for so long. It was a sacred place! To think violence and turmoil had taken it over hurt Rooper, even though she'd never visited herself.

There was even a witness claiming an unknown creature was at the center of it. It sounded like a monster. Rooper had faced monsters before—the poor corrupted Katikoots on Gloam, who'd attacked Dass and his father, along with anyone else who'd gotten in their way. It hadn't been their fault, but Rooper had still needed to fight them. She couldn't help wondering if this unknown creature on Jedha was similar. Maybe it only wanted something nobody knew how to give it.

The holonet report mentioned some kind of cult had been involved—maybe Force users, maybe not—called the Path of the Open Hand. They had claimed some responsibility, but maybe it had been a splinter group. . . . It was messy, and confusing.

Rooper wished she'd been there, at her master's side. She'd chosen to remain on Batuu and let Master Silandra go on her pilgrimage alone, but in retrospect she felt guilty for not having been where the danger was. Startled, Rooper realized that guilt might be one of the reasons she had so quickly agreed to leave Batuu with Dass and Sky.

Guilt was something she needed to let go of. Allow it to pass through her and stop affecting her choices.

Rooper breathed deeply and reminded herself she was where she needed to be. The Force wanted her with Sky and Dass. Guilt might have played a part, but she was listening to the Force. She was trying to. That was what she needed to do. Trust the Force.

Near the end of the hyperspace jump, the *Brightbird* alerted them they'd be coming out of hyperspace shortly. The three of them tromped to the cockpit. Sky glanced thoughtfully at Dass but took the pilot's seat.

Dass settled in at the navicomputer. Rooper took the comms station.

The ship dropped out of hyperspace.

Before them was a planet with huge bluish oceans and a handful of moons. Dass tapped a few buttons and said, "This is the far edge of the Tybal system. That's Imena, the only inhabited planet in the system, and it has five moons. One has a spaceport on it."

Sky said, "Why isn't the machine working? This isn't Planet X."

"Do they have any hyperspace lanes out here?" Rooper asked. She didn't think so. She'd read about this system in her research on Batuu.

"I'm not even detecting a beacon," Sky complained as they continued to scan the system.

Rooper looked out the viewport.

"Wait," Sky said. "They do have a Republic comms buoy. It's on the fritz."

Dass said, "I . . . think I've been here."

Sky spun to him. "When? Why?"

"It was a while ago. . . ." Dass frowned. He looked down at his lap.

"Is it connected to Planet X?" Rooper asked. "If it is, maybe that's why."

Dass shook his head. "I don't think so. Except that I was here, and I was there. This is where . . ."

Rooper reached out to grasp his shoulder. She squeezed.

"We were here right before we met Sunshine Dobbs," Dass admitted. "We fueled up planetside and went out that afternoon. It brings back good memories."

Rooper heard Sky suck in a soft breath, but when she glanced over, Sky was staring resolutely out the viewport. "Let's do another jump," Sky said firmly.

Dass nodded. "I'm up for it."

"Wait." Rooper stood. "I want to try to send another message. Since there's a buoy here, I can set up a relay."

"We don't have time—" Sky started, but Rooper squeezed their shoulder.

"We do," Rooper said.

Huffing a sigh, Sky flicked a few switches and took manual control of the drive stick to angle the *Brightbird*'s flight toward the comms buoy.

Sitting back at the comms station, Rooper pushed the channel button to make contact with the buoy. When pinged, it would reply with its designation number and the buoy network it was connected to. So Rooper would be able to tell which system she could contact through the relay. If the buoy was fully functional, that is. More often than not, they struggled along at around sixty or seventy percent.

Instead of a reply from the buoy, though, a voice crackled through the comms speaker. "Unknown vessel, this is the *Way of Clarity*. This comms buoy is under system repair."

Rooper sat up straight. "Hello," she responded. "This is Jedi Padawan Rooper Nitani on board the *Brightbird*. I was hoping to send a message to the Batuu system or toward Jedha."

"Ah, *Brightbird*, at this time your request is not possible. We're looking at a few more hours, and we might have to trade out the whole buoy."

Disappointed, Rooper tried not to sound it. "Understood. I'd like to leave a message with you, to be relayed once the buoy is back in operation."

"Can do, *Brightbird*. And actually . . ." The speaker seemed to hesitate, then said, "My name is Fel Ix, and we've hit a bit of a snag. I was wondering if you have a hydropick or even an all-tool? Ours got fried, and this little astromech unit over here hasn't been refitted for the newer hardware."

Dass said, "There's a set of picks in the toolbox in the engineering ladder well. Or probably they could use a refined fusioncutter."

"If they want to melt the internal brains of the buoy," Sky sneered.

"Listen," Dass said, "once I helped my dad rerig a fusioncutter with just a sliver of durasteel to interrupt the friction generator—"

Rooper tuned them out and said, "*Way of Clarity*, we do have a hydropick, several actually."

"Great news," the speaker, Fel Ix, said. "Do you mind if we hook up and borrow one? Then we can get this buoy fixed up and you can send your message."

"That's fine," Rooper said with a bright smile. "We'll be there in a few minutes. Will send docking codes." She glanced at the ident tab of the comms repair ship. They didn't appear to be an official Republic communications team, but they must have been nearby when the buoy went down. Rooper had worked with various Republic and non-Republic comms teams before, when she was traveling with Master Silandra. The teams usually followed Pathfinders to place buoys just like this one in a big network, to improve communications on the frontier They broke down a lot. It was a work in progress—like everything out there.

"Here it is, Rooper," Sky said, and Rooper looked out the viewport.

The comms buoy was about twice as long as she was tall if she counted the cluster of long sensors sticking out the bottom. It was shaped like a dome with multiple lenses, and a comms dish tilted off the top like a little cap. The buoy was totally dwarfed by the ship moving toward the *Brightbird*. The *Way of Clarity* looked like a typical comms ship, with two big engines giving it hyperspace capabilities, on either side of a narrow crew space and a tall hold for extra buoys. Several comms dishes were aimed toward different parts of the stars. This ship had no extra markings, beyond what looked like identification numbers across the nose.

"Ready to connect," the *Way of Clarity* said.

"Are you sure about this?" Sky asked.

"They need help," Rooper said. It was a Jedi's duty to help those they could.

Sky pursed their lips but signaled that they were accepting the docking codes from the other ship. It took only a few minutes, and Rooper felt a soft shudder through the *Brightbird*'s frame and heard the clang of the airlock snapping into place.

Dass rushed past Rooper. "I'll grab the kit from the ladder well!" he called.

Rooper followed more sedately, and Sky said, "I'll be with you shortly."

Rooper checked that her lightsabers were in place and grabbed her cloak from the galley. She buckled it over her shoulders. Quickly combing her fingers through her hair, she caught it in a tail and tied it back, leaving her Padawan braid free against her neck. She needed to present the most competent front as a representative of the Jedi.

The airlock was on the other side of the galley, not on the hold level where the boarding ramp was, and Rooper stood with her hands clasped lightly before her. The lights on the panel changed to blue, indicating the airlock was pressurized and ready to open. Rooper reached out and hit the go switch.

Just as the door hissed open, Dass popped up beside her, a large black toolbox hugged to his chest. He had a smudge of something on his cheek—hydraulic oil, it looked like. Rooper smiled fondly. Then they turned to face the incoming party.

Three people stepped onto the *Brightbird*: a lithe green-gray Kessarine in a loose black jumpsuit, flanked by a human woman and a stout Ardennian with four arms.

Dass said, "Hi! I'm Dass Leffbruk. Welcome to the *Brightbird*."

The Kessarine nodded but kept his golden eyes on Rooper. His cheek furls were held tight to his face. "You are the Jedi. I am Fel Ix. Thank you for letting us onto your ship."

Something about the way he said it made Rooper uneasy. Nothing about them looked like a comms team, even an unofficial one. She smiled calmly, reaching out to the Force with her question. "Of course. It's important to work together to further communications in the galaxy."

Fel Ix didn't move for a moment, studying her. Rooper sensed tension through the Force, like the three guests had a huge weight hanging over them. Then Fel Ix simply nodded at her.

Dass held out the toolbox. The human woman reached forward and took it, using its weight to pull Dass off balance.

Rooper stepped forward, but not in time to stop Fel Ix from grabbing Dass's arm with a long-fingered hand and pulling a blaster out of a holster in the small of his back. He aimed it at Dass.

CHAPTER THIRTEEN

Dass stared wide-eyed at the muzzle of the blaster aimed at his ribs. His heart leapt, and he didn't know what to do. So he held still, not jerking away from the Kessarine even though he really, really wanted to.

"I'm very sorry," Fel Ix said to Rooper in a soft, gravelly voice. "I need you to put your lightsaber on the deck and kick it over to me."

"Rooper, d—" Dass couldn't say it. He wanted to tell her to fight, or run, but he couldn't. Fear stiffened his whole body.

"It's okay, Dass," Rooper said quietly.

He flicked his wide eyes toward her, trying not to get any closer to the blaster. He couldn't believe the comms team was acting like this—except he could. It was just how people were on the frontier. You couldn't trust anybody! Dass was surprised, suddenly, that Sky hadn't betrayed them yet.

Rooper had one hand out flat, and with the other she unlatched the lightsaber on her right hip.

Only that one.

The other lightsaber was hidden under the fall of her Jedi cloak.

Dass tried not to look at it, his gaze snapping back to Rooper.

"Now kick it over here," the Kessarine, Fel Ix, said, tightening his fingers painfully around Dass's arm.

Suddenly, Dass's frustration and fear poured out, and he yelled, "What do you want?"

Fel Ix glanced down at him. The green ruffles on his high cheeks twisted a little bit.

"We're just a prospecting ship," Dass said, breathing hard. Maybe if he could keep their attention, Rooper could . . .

"Jedi don't belong on a prospecting ship," Fel Ix said.

Rooper sucked in a surprised breath.

"What!" Dass yelled. "Jedi are part of Pathfinder teams."

Fel Ix pulled Dass with him as the Kessarine backed up. "Char, pick up that lightsaber. Rooper Nitani, find something to bind your hands."

"Are you trying to kidnap Rooper?" Dass exclaimed. That was a ridiculous idea. The Jedi would be after her in no time.

"Quiet," Fel Ix said. He wrenched Dass around, and Dass had to bite his lip to keep from crying out.

Rooper glared at Fel Ix, her jaw set. "Let him go."

"Tie yourself up or I will hurt him," Fel Ix said.

Reluctantly, Rooper backed into the galley.

"Look around," Fel Ix ordered his crew. The human and Ardennian moved immediately, opening panels and digging through pots and game pieces. Rooper stood close to the hatch leading into the cockpit, but angled with her back against an access panel. Dass thought she was stalling and trying to find a better position to leverage her remaining lightsaber.

Fel Ix narrowed his big yellow eyes. "What is taking so long, Jedi?"

"It's not my ship. I don't know where everything is," Rooper said as she stepped closer to the Kessarine.

Dass widened his eyes at her and kept his hands out to his sides. Rooper glanced at him and pressed her lips together in a grim smile. She nodded. Okay, she did have a plan. He just had to be ready.

"If it is not your ship," Fel Ix said softly, "what are you doing here? Why would a Jedi be here, one of two children, and not the ship's owner? Do not tell me this fancy cruiser belongs to this child."

"Jedi have a lot of missions. We're here to help however we can. And I'm here helping my friend."

"Without your master?"

How did he know— Dass gaped at Rooper, but Rooper lifted her chin. "I'm where the Force wills me to be."

Fel Ix smiled then. "So am I. So are we all, here to serve the Force."

Rooper narrowed her eyes. "You don't serve the Force."

"We do. We protect it from its abusers—like the Jedi."

"That's ridiculous!" Dass said.

"Jedi don't abuse the Force," Rooper said, still angling nearer. Behind Dass the other two crew members from Fel Ix's ship continued making noise as they searched the galley and lounge.

Fel Ix shrugged one shoulder, moving toward the cockpit hatch. "Why else did the Force abandon the Jedi on Jedha when the great Leveler returned harmony to the Force?"

Rooper's whole body seemed to lock up. She shook her head. "You don't know what you're talking about."

"Rooper Nitani," Fel Ix said. His cheek furls flickered. "I know you believe Jedi are good. I know you trust the Force, however wrongly you have been taught. You aren't the first Padawan I have known."

Where was Sky? Dass wondered. What if they were on Fel Ix's side now because the Kessarine had the upper hand? Suddenly, he thought of the resonance machine and that Rooper used the Force to move the lodestone. Maybe they could leverage it as an artifact for Fel Ix to take and leave them alone! But Sky might not agree.

Where had Sky gone?

"I . . ." Rooper suddenly flicked out her right hand and

threw herself forward. The blaster tore free of Fel Ix's grip and went flying toward Rooper. Dass lunged away. He hit the deck hard on his shoulder and rolled, then scrambled up just as he heard a yell from the Ardennian and the vivid hiss-hum of a lightsaber.

The ship seemed to spin around him a little, but Dass was only dizzy. He turned to look, wishing he had a weapon. But Rooper had her lightsaber a breath away from Fel Ix's neck, her other hand twisted in his long head frills.

The Kessarine's tiny scales shone in the blue light of Rooper's lightsaber.

Both the human and Ardennian crew members had frozen.

Rooper said, "Get off our ship, now! Don't make me use this."

Dass stared. Rooper couldn't do something like that! But she had said it so calmly.

Fel Ix blinked. His cheek furls were tight against his face. He moved one hand out flat toward his crew. "She won't. I told you I have known a Padawan before, and she won't kill me. Not like this."

"I will, to protect my friends," Rooper said. She tugged at Fel Ix's thin head frills, craning his neck back.

"Fel Ix," urged the human woman.

But without moving his head, Fel Ix rolled his big yellow eyes so he was looking at Rooper. "If you must kill me, it is the will of the Force," he said, almost gently. Like he forgave her already.

Rooper's lips trembled. Her lightsaber remained steady—a constant, pure line of blue, glinting in the Kessarine's eyes. "Who are you?" Rooper asked. "How can you be so sure of the Force but . . ."

"Resist Jedi?" Fel Ix finished for her.

The Ardennian snarled, "Jedi do not know the Force like the Path does."

"The Path?" Rooper gasped.

"You can come with us to learn, Padawan," Fel Ix coaxed. "We are the Path of the Open Hand, and we welcome all who come to the Force seeking clarity, harmony, and freedom. With open hands." He turned both his hands over, palms up.

Dass wished he could think of what to do. Behind him,

from the hatch leading to the cockpit, he heard a slow, soft hydraulic hiss. He knew that sound!

"Your open hands came carrying blasters," Dass said loudly, to draw everyone's attention.

All but Rooper looked at him, which was great. They weren't looking at what was causing the hiss.

Rooper released Fel Ix's frills but kept her lightsaber close to his face and neck. "I won't go with you."

"But no matter how wrong you are about the Force, you are a Jedi, and you won't kill me," Fel Ix said. "So we are at an impasse."

Blaster fire shrieked past Dass and hit the Ardennian in the shoulder. They howled, clutching their wound. Rooper didn't move, and Fel Ix's body went rigid as he stared beyond Dass into the cockpit.

"I'm not a Jedi," Sky said as the cannon nest lift finished its corkscrew down. Sky held a blaster of their own, aimed at Fel Ix. "I'm a Graf, and if you've heard of my family, you know I'm not afraid to use my blaster on the likes of you."

CHAPTER FOURTEEN

"Sky," Rooper breathed. She lowered her lightsaber but held it so the tip was still aimed at Fel Ix.

Sky hopped out of the cannon nest, their boots slamming hollowly onto the steel deck. "Hey, Rooper. Miss me?" They kept their face stern, even when Rooper smiled her relief.

Gesturing with the blaster, Sky said, "So you two slimeballs get going. We'll send this one right behind."

Rooper let Sky take over but kept her attention on Fel Ix. Her heart pounded, and she did her best to regulate her breathing. It made her hand steadier. "Give me back my other lightsaber, too," she said.

Fel Ix's mouth turned down on one side, acknowledging he'd been fooled by her double blades. "Do as they say."

The human woman moved to the Ardennian, who continued to softly groan and hold their shoulder. She nudged the Ardennian, and they winced but held up the lightsaber. Rooper said, "Roll it on the floor toward Dass."

The handle clicked repeatedly as it rolled across the deck.

Dass picked it up. "I got it, Rooper."

"Good." Rooper stepped back, still holding her lightsaber up. Her arm was beginning to ache slightly. She focused on the Force and held steady.

Sky said, "Dass, head up to the cockpit and start the navicomputer. I want to get out of here."

"Will do, Sky." Dass saluted with Rooper's lightsaber and dashed up toward the cockpit.

"Now, you two," Sky said, striding nearer to Fel Ix and Rooper. "Off my ship."

Fel Ix added soothingly, "Start the decoupling process so that when I follow we can release immediately."

The two left, the Ardennian limping slightly even though the flesh wound was on their shoulder. The airlock gasped and hissed, and they went through.

"We should keep this one," Sky said.

Fel Ix bristled. His cheek fronds actually stiffened.

Rooper didn't look over her shoulder at Sky, though she wanted to. "I said we'd let them go."

"But what were they doing with the buoy?" Sky asked. "What does the Path of the Open Hand want with comms buoys, Rooper?"

"We don't have a way of containing him," Rooper hedged.

Sky frowned thoughtfully.

From the cockpit, Rooper heard the sounds of proximity alerts.

"Sky! That ship followed us!" Dass yelled. "The *Starlily*, from before! Your brother's ship! I'm trying to get coordinates ready for a jump, but I can't pilot at the same time!"

Sky and Rooper's eyes locked. Rooper said, "I've got Fel Ix. You get us out of here."

"We need you for the . . ." Sky stopped before giving away the existence of the machine . They gritted their teeth and said, "You have to be willing to use your lightsaber."

With that, Sky spun around and ran to help Dass.

Rooper grimaced but looked Fel Ix right in the eye. "I am willing," she said.

Fel Ix bowed his head.

"Get over there and hit the airlock controls. Uncouple now."

Fel Ix moved and did as she said. Then he lifted one hand to one of the many pockets of his black jumpsuit. "May I call my ship?"

"Just tell them to—"

The *Brightbird* lurched sideways.

Rooper threw her legs out to maintain balance, and Fel Ix managed the same. Then the compensators kicked in, and as the ship turned again and twisted, they both held on. "Call them," Rooper said. "Then toss the comlink in the recycler and sit down at that table. Hands flat."

Fel Ix hit the button on the small comlink. "Severn, I'm taking a trip with this Padawan. Continue the mission."

"Fel Ix . . ." The human woman's voice pushed through, sounding worried.

"Go," Fel Ix said. "The Force will be free."

Rooper sucked a breath through her teeth. The phrase filled her with *anger*—she couldn't help it. This Path did not understand the Force better than the Jedi! She needed to know what they'd done on Jedha and if—if Silandra was okay! "Throw it in the recycler," she commanded.

Fel Ix did so just as the ship turned fast. He sat on the bench behind the small galley table and pressed his long green-gray fingers flat on its surface.

Finally, Rooper flicked her lightsaber off. The hum vanished, and even though she'd barely noticed it the past few minutes, she felt its lack in her chest. She kept it in hand. Just in case.

A high whine sounded, and the *Brightbird* jolted. They were taking fire.

"Sit down back there!" Sky cried.

Rooper did not sit, but she moved to lean hard against the refrigerator panel and braced herself as best she could. She kept her focus on Fel Ix but let the Force flood through her. She welcomed the surety of its colors and comfort. She could do this.

Fel Ix closed his big golden eyes, and Rooper knew he was meditating. She felt the shift in the Force, because she was so focused on it and him. He wasn't Force-sensitive but fell into meditative energy almost as easily as blinking.

Distantly, she could hear Sky and Dass arguing, and the sound of lasers streaked past again. There was nothing she could do. They had the navigation and piloting down. Rooper could help by keeping Fel Ix there.

When the *Brightbird* dove sharply, Fel Ix's fingers tightened against the table. Rooper sheathed her lightsaber and held on.

The Force was part of her. She was part of the Force. She breathed.

Fel Ix opened his eyes suddenly, just before they felt the telltale jolt of the hyperspace engines kicking in. Then there was a pulling tremble and the moment of weightless relief as the *Brightbird* entered hyperspace.

CHAPTER FIFTEEN

Sky leaned their full weight against the control panel in the cockpit and turned wide eyes, unblinking, out to the streaks of hyperspace.

Adrenaline pulsed coldly through their whole body, and any moment now they'd start shaking. They did not want anybody to see, especially Dass. Or that prisoner Rooper was holding in the galley.

But today had been a lot.

When the *Way of Clarity* had docked with the *Brightbird*, Sky had hung back to let Rooper deal with it. Just in case.

Sky sure had been right, hadn't they?

It was good Sky knew about the blaster Helis had hidden behind a tiny panel under the pilot station, tangled in with blue and copper wires. The blaster held only enough charge to sting, but it would do in a pinch. Sky had grabbed it and slipped into the lift to the cannon nest. From the nest, they sliced into the ship's comms and listened. There was no way to see anything, but hearing gave them plenty of information. As soon as Rooper made her move, Sky was ready to back her up.

Sky didn't want to hurt anybody but didn't let that stop them. They had gritted their teeth and pulled the trigger, yelling big game about being a Graf.

Grafs were even better at bluffing than at shooting people.

Fortunately, it worked. Even more fortunately, Sky didn't have to kill anyone.

Then Dass had sounded the alarm from the cockpit and Sky had run in to find Dass half in the pilot's seat and half reaching for the navicomputer, trying to get it to spit out coordinates for a short escape jump.

"I've got the pilot station," Sky had said, and Dass immediately dropped out of the seat and hit his knees hard. He started keying in commands to the navicomputer. "Just two minutes," he said.

Sky focused on Helis, who had *followed them through hyperspace*, which was impossible unless he had a . . . Helis tried to break through the shields again, and Sky grabbed the thruster controls, glanced to make sure they were decoupled from the *Way of Clarity* enough not to tear a hole in the hull, and swung the *Brightbird* in a full circle—then dove.

"Ahh!" Dass cried.

"Sorry," Sky said through a grimace. "Got those coordinates yet?"

"Almost!"

They were far from any occlusions, so Sky just had to keep the other ship behind them, but not directly behind them where they'd be an easy target! Sky wanted to curse but didn't have the breath.

Target lock, the *Brightbird* display read, and Sky wheeled them around once more. The shield array took the hit, but more lasers whined past the viewport. "Sit down back there!" Sky yelled over their shoulder, hoping Rooper was all right. "Dass?" they urged.

"Ten seconds!" Dass's hands flew over the controls.

The navicomputer spit out its reading, and Sky said, "Hit it when you're ready. We're clear."

Dass didn't need to be told twice. The kid pulled on the lever immediately.

Sky barely bit back the shout of joy and relief they felt when the star field blurred and then smoothed into the bright simu-tunnel of hyperspace.

They leaned into the pilot's station, shoulders heaving as they breathed hard.

Dass sighed heavily, too.

"You okay, Dass?"

"Yeah. Yeah, great. Totally fine." Dass bent over the navicomputer. His lanky twelve-year-old body was all limbs and floppy hair. "How did they follow us?" he asked, his voice muffled against the metal.

"There's only one way I know of," Sky said. They picked themself up and stood, then touched an icon and saw the jump would take nearly half a day. Everything was so far away on the frontier.

"A tracker," Dass said darkly.

"A tracker," Sky agreed. "Let's have a ship meeting in the galley."

They joined Rooper and the Kessarine. Sky dug into one of the narrow drawers and came out with some thick plastic twine. They took it and lifted their eyebrows at Fel Ix. He moved his hands together, and Sky tied him up, tightening the twine enough to press slightly against the little green scales on his wrist bones. Fel Ix leaned back on the bench and said nothing.

"What happened?" Rooper asked, accepting her light-saber back from Dass. It had been in one of the looping pockets of his coverall pants.

"My brother tracked us," Sky answered as Dass plopped down a half meter from Fel Ix. Sky grabbed an expandable chair and flicked it into shape. They turned it and sat with their arms crossed over the back.

Rooper frowned. "That . . . shouldn't be possible."

"If they put a tracker in the ship it is," Dass said. "And if there were comms buoys—working ones—where we stopped, the buoy could relay a short burst pretty fast."

"But fast is the problem," Sky said. "They were on us less than an hour after we got here."

"Not enough time to receive a signal and jump from

wherever they were to where we were," Rooper said, completing the thought.

All three of them were on the same page.

Fel Ix closed his eyes as if he planned to take a nap.

"I don't . . . I don't think there was a buoy the first time." Dass tapped his fingers on the table. "It was totally uninhabited, wasn't it?"

"Then it can't be a tracker," Rooper said.

Sky unfocused their eyes, staring into the middle distance as they thought. It was possible Helis had some very fancy new kind of tracker, but without comms buoys, there'd be nothing to relay the information. Sky sank into thought, counting all the ways they knew of to track somebody in space. There weren't very many, and all involved trackers, system breaches, or—

Sky sat up straight. "The navicomputer." They flung themself back to the cockpit and cued up a systems diagnostic.

Dass and Rooper followed. "What are you looking for?"

"Helis is an engineer, and he really gets math, so he uses complex equations far more than most people. I know them, because I worked with him on most of them. Plus we have—our family has—a system of codes we can use as a secret language. Helis designed this whole ship—I helped, but Helis is the one who had his hands in the navicomputer. And then he sliced in at Travyx Prime. He got into the ship itself. That's how he could control things."

"I didn't even know you could do that," Dass murmured, sounding as shocked as Sky felt.

Rooper nodded agreement. "I thought you had to be in physical contact to slice a security system. Or have a spy droid or something as an intermediary."

Sky said, "I don't think it would be possible except Helis built the ship's systems. He could have put anything he wanted into the codes—and only he could slice in. Maybe I could . . ." Sky moved to the pilot station and started a whole ship-wide diagnostic while they were at it. "Who's watching Fel Ix?"

Rooper said, "I used one of the ties to bind him to a cable loop in the wall. He can't go anywhere."

Dass took over the ship-wide diagnostic while Sky dug into the navicomputer readouts. It seemed correct, except—there, a little command worked into the jump sequence to bundle the calculations into a data burst and then . . .

"Poodoo," Sky snarled.

"You found it?"

"Yeah. The navicomputer itself betrayed us. When we jump it drops a tight data burst with the codes for our route! So as long as Helis is there to pick up the data, he can follow us to the next location. Helis is so sneaky. I can extract the command, but . . ." Sky shook their head. "I don't see how I can do that without a system shutdown to bring it all back in line with my own codes. I'll have to strip the Graffian. Our family codes. And re-input the correct ones. Which means—"

"We have to land somewhere we don't need life support," Dass said sulkily.

Rooper asked, "Where are we going now?"

"A mining colony I remember stopping at with my dad. They'll have a dock, but—"

"But Helis has the data," Sky said. "He knows where we're going."

"What's the nearest planet or moon to the mining colony that would work?"

After replacing the panel, Sky asked the navicomputer.

It took only a moment to locate such a place relative to their coordinates. "An unnamed moon in the Farj system," Sky said. "We'll get the coordinates as ready as we can, and when we come out of hyperspace at the mining colony we'll jump immediately. Hopefully, Helis won't be close enough behind us to catch the data burst."

"The Farj system is uninhabited. I don't know details about the moon, but the system has three planets and a bright sun," Rooper said, like a walking encyclopedia.

Dass smiled. "You've heard of it."

"I did a lot of reading about the various planets along the frontier after being caught unawares on Gloam."

"Good idea," the kid said.

"I wonder why it's uninhabited then," Sky said, mostly just out of curiosity.

Rooper looked at Sky with big brown eyes. "No water."

"Good thing we don't have to survive there long. Just enough time to fix up the *Brightbird*."

CHAPTER SIXTEEN

The route to Farj would take several hours.
They all needed a rest.

But they had to do something with Fel Ix.

Rooper suggested the refresher. It was contained. There
was no easy access to anything that could be sabotaged.

Then Dass asked quietly, "What if we have to use the
toilet?"

Sky groaned.

They couldn't put their prisoner in the engine hold,
which was also contained and easy to lock down. The

Kessarine could easily mess something up in there. Same for the cockpit.

Sky pressed their hands to their face, clearly regretting keeping Fel Ix. Rooper agreed. But it was too late now. "We could put him in the bunks?"

"Feel free to keep me right here," Fel Ix suggested.

In the galley.

Sky rolled their eyes. Dass shrugged. Rooper sighed.

So that was what they did.

Rooper claimed to feel rested already, because she'd been able to meditate. What she really wanted, though, was to talk with Fel Ix about the Path of the Open Hand, and Jedha.

Dass and Sky took the chance to get some sleep while Rooper sat in the galley with Fel Ix. The *Brightbird* was set to alert her if she was needed in the cockpit.

Rooper made two cups of a tea she found in tiny cubbies set under the water unit. The cups felt like real stone in her fingers. Delicate, shallow, but with the weight of a planet in their pale green lines.

Bringing them to the table, she pushed one close

enough that Fel Ix could take it between the fingers of his bound hands.

Then Rooper sat across from him and stared. She tried to look confident, and maybe a little intimidating. She sipped her tea once the steam had calmed down. She let the warmth, as it infused her throat and stomach, be like the Force—spreading through her body, her awareness. The Kessarine was part of it, too, and perfectly at ease, it seemed. Either he had nothing to lose, or he was a very good actor. Or he trusted the Force as much as Rooper did.

Fel Ix lifted the tea and sipped it, too. His cheek furls rippled as he met Rooper's gaze. A set of inner eyelids blinked, startling her. The Kessarine smiled with one side of his mouth.

Rooper had so many questions about the Path of the Open Hand, about what he'd called a Leveler, about the Battle of Jedha and what the Path wanted from the Jedi. She didn't want to just start demanding answers but to make this more of a conversation. "Tell me about the Path," she said gently.

Fel Ix tilted his head. "What do you wish to know?"

Tamping down frustration, she answered, "What do you believe?"

"We believe that the Force is everything, part of everything. And that it is sacred. Using it to influence thoughts, emotions, or the material world hurts its balance, and that has consequences."

"So you mean that when I used the Force to take your blaster, there will be a consequence for that?"

"Somewhere." Fel Ix nodded. "You may never know what, or how it affects the galaxy."

Rooper knew that wasn't how the Force worked. It was infinite, constant. Taking here didn't deprive people there. She also wasn't very interested in arguing about it. "Why does the Path want to hurt Jedi?"

"That is not what we want. We want you to stop abusing the Force, not to hurt you."

"Why the Jedi? There are other Force users. Sorcerers of Tund. The Lonto."

Fel Ix nodded. "We want everyone to stop. Everyone should. But the Jedi are the most powerful, and the most organized, of those who abuse the Force. Only in leaving the Force alone, only in allowing the Force to be free, can there be true balance."

"You think you're protecting the Force from . . . us." Rooper couldn't help the disbelief in her voice.

"You don't have to believe me," Fel Ix said. "But when you face the Leveler, you will know. You will see the true nature of the Force, and how devastating it can be to those who are its enemies."

A chill shook Rooper. She breathed deeply. The Force was with her. "The Jedi are not the enemy of the Force."

"The Leveler believes you are."

"What is the Leveler?" The rumors from Jedha had been so strange. Abrupt violence, rioting, and a few hints about some kind of glowing monster that attacked Force users. Attacked them and caused panic. Rooper wished she'd had a chance to speak with Master Silandra about it. Any of it. She wished she could convince Sky and Dass to take the *Brightbird* and find Silandra. The next time they reached a system with a comms buoy, she'd send another message.

"Our Mother, the leader of the Path, says the Leveler

is an avatar of the Force," Fel Ix said. "From a planet made material by the Force itself."

"A planet made . . ." Rooper suddenly felt a flash of insight. "Planet X. It's . . . a Force nexus. That's why everyone says it heals, is strange and beautiful, and . . ."

Fel Ix shook his head. "I do not know about that. I only know the Leveler was a gift to the Mother and the Path from the Force."

"How?" Rooper leaned over the table.

Fel Ix remained silent.

"Is the planet a dangerous place?" she asked.

"I do not know."

"That's where we're going. Dass has been there. Dass is taking us back to the planet."

"Others will have already come and gone," Fel Ix said with total certainty.

Rooper felt almost desperate to keep pushing at this conversation, as if being dragged by the Force to continue. She took a few more deep breaths. "Only Dass, his father, and Sunshine Dobbs have been there."

Fel Ix's golden eyes narrowed at the name Sunshine.

He knew Sunshine Dobbs. Maybe the prospector who'd

abandoned Dass and his father had sold the route to Planet X to the Path. Rooper couldn't believe this was all connected. But it was. The Force connected everything, and so, apparently, did Planet X. Did Master Silandra know? Did any of the Jedi Council? She had to contact them once they were out of hyperspace.

"How old are you?" Fel Ix asked.

She managed not to pout or glare. "Fifteen."

"Are you a child to your people still, Padawan?"

"I'm trusted to take care of myself and do my duty," she answered.

He smiled, and his cheek furls curled up in obvious amusement. But before she could snap back, his expression fell. It became almost sad. "You are young enough to save yourself. Leave the Jedi, and follow the Force in harmony, with clarity, and for freedom."

"Jedi serve the light, Fel Ix," Rooper said. "We help people. Saving myself isn't—isn't the priority."

"I see," he said. Then he nodded firmly. He lifted the teacup and finished every drop. "What are you going to do with me?"

It was a good question. Rooper wasn't certain. Maybe

keep Fel Ix until she could reunite with Master Silandra. Then Silandra could decide. Rooper did have the authority to hold him, because he had tried to kidnap Rooper at blaster-point. "What were you going to do with me, if I'd gone with you?"

"Take you to the Mother," Fel Ix said smoothly. "She would decide what to do with you."

Rooper studied him and wondered if he had been on the lookout for the *Brightbird.* Maybe Helis Graf had put out the word that his ship was stolen. "Did the Grafs tell you to look for us?"

"I do not work for the Grafs," Fel Ix said. "I do as I am asked by my leaders. By the Elders and the Mother."

"You're a grunt," she said. "A soldier for the Path."

He tilted his head in acknowledgment.

"But you know another Padawan."

Fel Ix lowered his gaze. "Knew."

Rooper sucked in a gasp.

It brought the Kessarine's golden gaze snapping back up to hers. He smiled sadly. "Yes. He is dead."

Rooper hadn't heard of any Padawans dying on the

frontier. Not recently. Not ever, maybe? Her stomach turned over. It could be a lie. "You're lying."

"I would like for that to be so," Fel Ix said. "He saved my children's lives. And that of my partner. The galaxy would be better with Kevmo Zink alive and doing as you say: saving people. But the Force did not will it. The Leveler took him, judged him. And he is dead."

As she listened, Rooper's body seemed to melt a little. She made her hands into fists in her lap, wishing to take out her lightsabers and ignite them. They would make her feel strong.

She wished she had Master Silandra's shield.

And Fel Ix sounded truly sorry.

Rooper whispered, "His name was Kevmo?"

"Kevmo Zink. He worked with a Jedi Master called Zallah Macri."

A frisson of grief cut through Rooper. She did her best to note it and let it go. Though Rooper had not met them, she'd heard their names. Silandra knew Zallah Macri, who was stationed at Port Haileap, and had met her Padawan. "Master Zallah is also dead?" she confirmed in a small voice.

"Yes, though I was not witness to it."

Rooper swallowed and leaned back. This was awful. She was not prepared for this sort of thing. Rooper tried to let the strong emotions she was feeling pass through her and leave only calm intention. Connection to the Force. She needed to meditate. She wanted Master Silandra. "But you did see Kevmo die? You didn't stop it? He saved your children, and your partner. Your family, you said."

Fel Ix studied her silently. He blinked with both sets of eyelids. "In the presence of the Leveler, there is no saving Jedi."

CHAPTER SEVENTEEN

They set the *Brightbird* down on the only continent on the small moon orbiting the second planet in the Farj system. It didn't have a name, and neither did the gas planet it revolved around. It was just an uninteresting moon without anything anybody particularly wanted.

Dass and his dad used to find places like it all the time.

Sky set them down lightly on what the scans said was a network of organic matter that spread across the surface of the continent like an aboveground root system. It seemed sturdy. The *Brightbird* held still as it would on solid rock.

"The atmosphere is safe for all of us," Sky said. "Why

don't you all go for a walk while I reboot. There won't be anything to do in here."

Dass's stomach twisted. He wanted to trust Sky. But it hadn't been very long since Sunshine abandoned him and his dad on Gloam. At the time, he'd liked Sunshine just fine, too. The stinky old prospector always had sweets, and told Dass outrageous stories when his dad wasn't listening.

Rooper hesitated. "Are there any communications in this system?"

"It's barely a system," Sky answered dismissively. "Just a private hyperspace beacon."

Rooper shot Sky a look Dass was familiar with: disapproval. Rooper had already argued against private lanes, and Dass had to admit he agreed with her—everybody should be able to go everywhere without paying huge fees to private families like the Grafs.

Before Rooper and Sky could get into it again and delay fixing the ship, Dass shifted closer to Rooper and said quietly, "Rooper, do you think . . . Sky isn't going to leave us here, are they?"

Rooper's eyebrows shot up on her forehead. She looked at Sky. "I don't . . . no." The Padawan took a deep breath, and when she closed her eyes and stretched out her fingers, Dass was pretty sure she was making it obvious she was listening to the Force. For him. To make him feel better.

He could do this. He had chosen Sky, days earlier, and had to trust them. He trusted Rooper. Sky needed him, too, didn't they? The Graf astro-resonance machine worked only with Dass. "It's all right, Rooper," he said. "I'm all right."

Opening her eyes, she studied Dass for a moment.

Sky cleared their throat. Without looking at anyone, they said, "Do you want to take the combustion resonator? It's pretty easy to pry out of the engine, and I can't take off without it."

Feeling a little guilty, and squirming with thanks that Sky understood, Dass reached out and touched Sky's arm. "No, I don't need it. We'll go explore."

Rooper nodded. "Let us know as soon as you're done," she said. Sky patted the pocket containing their comlink.

Dass hurried past Rooper, headed toward his bunk. But as he dashed through the galley, he slowed down, watching the Kessarine hostage. Fel Ix slouched on the cushioned bench behind the table, eyes closed. His long-fingered hands were folded together, looking very relaxed in spite of the twine binding his wrists.

"Should we take him with us?" Dass asked.

Rooper frowned. "Let him stretch his legs, too. And use the refresher. Yes, I suppose we should."

Dass continued to his bunk and grabbed his macrobinoculars and utility hat. He settled the hat on the back of his head so it peeked over the goggles pushed up in his hair. The macrobinoculars he clipped to his jacket. Dass patted himself down, making sure he had all the other essentials still. Rope, multi-tool, comlink, grapple extender, and the little kit that would let him analyze water and take samples of minerals and dirt. Not that he'd need that.

When he came back out, Rooper was waiting in the hold with Fel Ix beside her, his hands still bound.

"Ready?" Rooper asked.

Dass nodded emphatically.

She punched in the code to release the boarding ramp. The *Brightbird* acknowledged the request with a pretty trill of beeps, and the door swished open over the lowering ramp.

Fel Ix stepped down without hesitating, and Rooper followed, a hand on one of her lightsabers.

Dass smiled. Even though this was a detour and slowing them down in finding the *Silverstreak* on Planet X, he loved this part of prospecting. It could only have been better if his father were there—and his mother, too. Dass wished he hadn't had to grow up without her.

The atmosphere around the moon gave the sky a cloudless, streaky quality, blue-green to Dass's eye. His boots sank into the ground. It was a little spongy. He bounced slightly in place as he glanced around. Behind him, he heard the *Brightbird* powering down.

The root system that covered the ground was silver and gray, with stripes of blue in places, and every once in a while the roots reached up and formed big mushroom fans. Here and there specks floated in the air, probably seeds of some kind, Dass thought. It was strange that it was so uniform, compared with a forest of obviously diverse trees and grasses and flowers, or even a grassland that looked the same from a distance but contained different individual plants.

"I think this is one big organism," Rooper said, reaching to touch the edge of the nearest mushroom fan.

"Will it eat us?" Fel Ix asked.

"I . . . don't think so." Rooper's eyes were closed, but then she snapped them open to keep an eye on the Kessarine. "It feels like it's minding its own business."

"Does it care we landed a ship on it?" Dass asked.

Rooper smiled. "I'm not sure it's even noticed us, really. But we should be careful."

Dass nodded. He moved farther from Rooper and Fel Ix, though not too far. "Dad and I would probably spend the night in a place like this, ready to go at a moment's notice. Maybe play some music or talk to it, or flash different lights to see if there was any reaction to us. Nothing harmful. My mom . . ." Dass took a deep breath before continuing. "Mom was an amateur biologist and liked to map out organic systems like this. At least get enough data to categorize the life. If it didn't seem dangerous, we'd take a few samples. Dad and I kept doing it, even after she died. I hope he's not too angry with me."

Dass bit his lip. He remembered the strain in Spence's voice when they'd briefly talked at Travyx. He hated to worry his dad, but this was what he wanted to be doing! Piloting a ship through hyperspace, exploring, working with the Jedi—it was like being on a Pathfinder team all his own. By reaching Planet X and getting the *Silverstreak* back, he'd prove to his dad he was ready to take charge of his future. Maybe that would make it easier to tell his dad what he wanted.

"I do not know your father," Fel Ix said softly. "But I would be more worried than angry. At least until my wayward child was safe again."

"You have kids?" Dass said. The Kessarine didn't seem old enough to have kids. "How old are you?"

"Nineteen. It is old enough for my people. But my children are . . . new. Fresh hatchlings," Fel Ix said. "They are with the rest of the Path on the *Gaze Electric*, with their other parents."

Dass hoped they were able to let Fel Ix get back to his little ones, eventually.

"Isn't it dangerous to have your families with you like that?" Rooper said. "While you start this—whatever it is—against the Jedi?"

Dass looked at the Kessarine, who flicked the fronds

on his right cheek. He said, "A family is safest when it is together."

That felt right to Dass, and his chest warmed—even though his dad wasn't there.

Rooper didn't answer. Dass kept wandering, craning his head to look up at the curled edge of a mushroom fan. It seemed like the color changed slightly, a subtle gradient from gray to a dark pink. This place wasn't exactly beautiful, but Dass liked it. It was weird and calm. Quiet.

Behind him, he heard Fel Ix say, "You should unbind my wrists. It will be safer."

Rooper kept quiet, probably glaring.

Fel Ix continued, "You have your lightsabers. I have no weapon, no communicator, and no incentive to attempt an escape right now."

It made sense to Dass. But his attention was caught by a slight bulge in the root network ahead of him. He crouched. It was just a little round hill, about the size of his head. Dass touched it very lightly. It shimmied beneath his finger. The root tendrils everywhere were tiny, more like filaments or delicate wires, but there they wove tighter together, maybe.

Dass spread his hand against the mound. He didn't push at all, just rested his hand there.

The filaments rippled, and Dass jerked his hand back just as the mound exploded, spraying him with liquid.

CHAPTER
EIGHTEEN

Rooper had just cut Fel Ix's bindings when she heard a startled cry and splatter.

She turned, along with Fel Ix, just in time to see Dass stand up and shake out his hands. He was covered in goo.

"Ugh!" Dass said, turning. He wiped at his face, but the goo seemed viscous. It stuck to him.

Rooper started closer. "Be careful. Don't let it get in your mouth or eyes."

The mushroom fan nearest Dass, about five meters away, suddenly shivered and turned so the broad side faced him.

"Uh-oh," Fel Ix said. "Dass, come this way."

The filament ground beneath Dass suddenly unwove itself, and Dass stumbled forward into a hole.

"Dass!" Rooper flung herself toward him, reaching with the Force. The whole place was lit up with colors through the Force, so bright Rooper had been slightly blocking it out. She hadn't been in tune with it, had been distracted by Fel Ix, and because of that she couldn't quite catch Dass.

Dass's scream was garbled as he was pulled underground by the root network. The roots wove themselves back together fast.

By the time Rooper and Fel Ix got to the spot where Dass had vanished, it was perfectly re-formed, as if there'd never been a hole. "Dass!" Rooper cried, falling to her knees and pressing the filaments. She couldn't hear anything or see any movement.

Fel Ix dug into the filaments with his strong fingers, clawing at them. He grunted as he tore them up. "It's tighter than iron sod," the Kessarine said.

Rooper grabbed one of her lightsabers but paused. She didn't want to hurt Dass. Closing her eyes, she reached out with everything she had and let the Force burst through her.

It was like standing on a silver sun, and Rooper struggled not to just bask in it. Dass. She needed to find him. She knew how he felt, the bright colors that made up his life.

Sweat broke out on her forehead as she felt her way through the vivid Force of the massive organism. But there—Dass was moving away from her.

She snapped open her eyes and looked. He was being pulled under the network toward the mushroom fan that had turned toward them. "There!" she pointed, flinging up to her feet. "It's taking him there."

Fel Ix ran.

Rooper followed. She could cut Dass free; she knew she could.

They reached the mushroom fan, and Fel Ix whirled. "Can you cut him out?"

"I have to concentrate," she said, "So I don't hurt him."

"You open it, I'll pull him out." Fel Ix's tone was firm. Confident.

Rooper nodded. She could do this. She didn't want to hurt this organism, but she had to. She had to get Dass.

Rooper squared her feet and focused. On the swirling colors of the Force, the even tranquility of this moon—except for what was right in front of her. There was the swirl of color she knew to be Dass. He moved slowly, as if doing something to stop himself. Good. "Keep it up, Dass," she murmured.

The hum of her lightsaber blazing to life surrounded her like a blanket. Without opening her eyes, only using the Force, she carefully pointed the lightsaber down and sliced into the network of tiny roots. She ignored the spike of guilt. The organism would be all right. This was important, and even if it hurt—she hoped it didn't—the moon would heal. Rooper felt hardly any resistance as she moved the lightsaber. She focused on Dass—if he began to travel faster, she'd have to stop.

"It's large enough," Fel Ix said.

Rooper shut off her lightsaber and looked.

The Kessarine was on his knees, an arm pushed into the tangle of roots all the way up to his shoulder.

Rooper released a deep breath and tried to keep breathing evenly.

"I have him." Fel Ix grunted as he pulled. Then Rooper saw the heel of Dass's boot.

She fumbled for her comlink. "Sky, are you almost done? We need to get back to the ship."

"Roger. I'm restarting all functions now."

"Good!"

"Is everything all right?" Sky's voice crackled. They sounded worried.

"I hope so," Rooper said as Fel Ix gave a great tug that pulled Dass more than halfway out. Rooper bent over, and instead of grabbing Dass, she grasped the side of the hole she'd made. It remained hot from the lightsaber, but not unbearably so. She leaned back with all her weight to help the hole expand.

Fel Ix pulled, and Dass popped the rest of the way out. A little gush of goo came with him. Immediately, Fel Ix turned him onto his side and pressed open Dass's mouth.

That was all it took. Dass coughed wretchedly, curling around himself. Rooper slumped in relief but rubbed Dass's back and pushed hair out of his eyes. He was sticky and coated in the viscous pink goo. It smelled sweet. Almost tangy. Where she pushed his hair away, Rooper could see Dass's skin was slightly abraded.

"Dass?" she said.

He nodded, then brought shaky hands up to rub goo out of his eyes.

Fel Ix sat back on his heels, studying Dass but no longer touching him. Rooper bit her lip and didn't say anything.

Dass sat up suddenly, wiping at his face. "That was so gross!"

Fel Ix huffed, almost like a laugh. "We should get back to the ship."

"Rooper?" Dass turned and looked at her, eyes wide and mouth hanging open a bit.

She smiled. "You're okay?"

"Slimy. So slimy. Thanks. You saved me."

"Fel Ix helped," she said, flicking her gaze at the Kessarine. Fel Ix's arms were gooey, too, and his cheek furls tightly twisted up with tension.

Dass turned fast enough that a splotch of goo flung off his hair and landed on Rooper's knee. She rubbed it off. It really was gross. And probably some kind of homing substance for the mushroom-fan thing.

"Let's go," she said, pushing up. She reached to help Dass up, and so did Fel Ix.

The root system under their feet shuddered.

All three of them looked down, then after a heartbeat pause, they ran for the ship.

CHAPTER NINETEEN

Sky felt a deep satisfaction as the comms system flickered back to life, all the lights blinking in a Graffian code modeled after a song their father used to sing to them. That was Sky's personal algorithm confirmation. Sky was in complete control of the ship's system again. *Take that, Helis.*

Once he was over his anger, Helis might even be impressed.

Their comlink buzzed, and Rooper said, "Open the ship, Sky. Also maybe turn on the shower."

Sky frowned at the breathless tone of Rooper's voice but

keyed in the command. "Did you fall in a pile of bantha fodder?"

"More like mushroom bile, I think," Rooper said.

Sky grimaced. "I'm going to get us off this moon and jump us away just in case Helis did manage to snag the data blast back in the last system. He definitely won't be able to follow again. Once we're underway I'll meet you back there."

Rooper acknowledged, and Sky started up the navicomputer. They wished they could get Dass and Rooper up there to start the resonator and head straight back into their quest. But they'd do that next jump.

Once the *Brightbird* confirmed the bay doors were locked again, Sky took off. The silver-gray surface of the moon turned shadowed as they flew toward the nightside, and then the viewport gave way to only stars. Checking the navicomputer, Sky saw the best short jump to make was along the route between Dalna and Thelj, which they didn't like. But on the other hand, Helis might assume Sky would never head back that way. So Sky acknowledged the jump and, once they were out of the moon's gravitational field, hit it.

The little tug and tremble of entering hyperspace soothed them, and Sky flicked the switch to autopilot and went to find the others.

Rooper stood alone outside Sky's quarters. She looked a little worse for wear, but otherwise okay. Sky noticed that the occupied lights were on outside both the private shower for the captain and the one across the corridor meant to be shared by the rest of the crew.

"What happened?" Sky asked, eyeing the private shower, then swinging around to Rooper. A faint sweet-sour smell hung in the air despite the state-of-the-art filtration system.

"The organism on the moon tried to . . . eat Dass I think."

"Is he okay?"

"We got him out. He seems to think it was interesting. And gross." Rooper winced. Her lashes flickered as she looked down at the white floor. Her tan cheeks seemed flushed.

Sky wanted to pat her shoulder, or push some of the strings of black hair messily escaping her braids out of her face. "You got him out. Don't feel bad."

"I don't know if I could have done it by myself. Without Fel Ix's help."

"That doesn't matter, because you had it."

Rooper pressed her lips together. She stared at Sky for a moment, then nodded.

The crew shower door hissed open, and the Kessarine stood there. He was mostly dry, with his black jumpsuit undone to the waist and hanging behind him like a skirt. It showed off a scarred green-gray torso with lines of scales and prominent, sharp-looking ribs. Rooper slowly realized what she'd thought was a belt wound around his waist was actually a tail.

"The arms of my suit are still drying. I had to scrub the . . . goo," he said.

"I considered throwing Dass's jacket and pants away," Rooper answered.

Sky grimaced again. "I'll go make tea."

They escaped to the galley. By the time the tea was ready and four cups set out on the table, the rest were making their way in to join Sky. Dass was saying, ". . . had time to grab a sample. It was really great lubrication and maybe not as flammable as what we usually use in hydraulics?

But I guess it's still in the navicomputer, so we could go back if—"

"It stank so much," Rooper said with a laugh.

"That's true!" Dass shuddered. He sat and scooted around on the bench, closer to Sky. "That shower is great, by the way. I'm so clean you could eat off my shoulders or something."

Sky raised their eyebrows. Dass seemed weirdly unaffected by his brush with death. "Is this still adrenaline from almost being eaten?"

"Naw, I wasn't in danger. Not with Rooper. Not when I'm . . . you know, not alone." The kid smiled shyly at Rooper, who looked uncomfortable as she slid in beside Dass but clearly tried to smile reassuringly.

Fel Ix shrugged his suit back over his arms before sitting tentatively.

That was when Sky realized he wasn't cuffed anymore. "So what, did you join the team?" they said a little meanly.

"Sky," Rooper chided. "We can't keep him prisoner forever, or even through this whole mission."

"If you feel that way, why didn't you just leave him on the moon?"

At Sky's words, Dass sucked in a sharp breath. His eyes went huge and round.

Fel Ix said nothing.

Rooper tapped her hand on the table for Sky's attention. "Sky, he helped save Dass. I told you. He didn't have to. Besides, he doesn't have any weapons. And he . . . trusts the Force."

Sky's mouth dropped open. "He blasted his way onto my ship!"

"It was a necessity," Fel Ix said. "But it no longer is. We all want the same thing now."

"And that is?" Sky demanded.

"To get to the nameless planet."

All three kids stared at the Kessarine.

"Really?" Dass said. "You want to go to Planet X, too?"

Fel Ix nodded. "Some of my people are there, or on their way. I can reunite with them when we arrive."

Sky shook their head. "No way. What's to stop you from reuniting and then using your greater numbers to try and take over my ship again?"

For some reason, Fel Ix looked at Rooper. She said, "Are your people going there for more of the monsters?"

"I am not privy to their plans. Only to my orders, which do not include harming the three of you."

"Yet," Sky said.

Rooper studied Fel Ix for a long moment and then looked at Sky. "We should trust his words for now, Sky."

Sky studied the three of them, sitting across the table together. They didn't have a lot of choice here and wanted to trust Rooper—wanted to trust Dass. But frankly, that wasn't how Grafs did things.

"Bind me again if you must," the Kessarine said.

"Let's do that," Sky bit out. Then they looked at Dass. "And it won't be long before we come out of hyperspace. Are you ready to try the resonance machine again?"

Dass nodded immediately, but Rooper said, "Wait."

"Why?"

Rooper straightened her shoulders and lifted her chin like she wanted to be taller sitting down. "I need to go back to Batuu. Or Jedha. I need to contact Master Silandra."

"But, Rooper," Dass cried, "you just agreed with Fel Ix that we all want to go to Planet X."

Rooper looked regretfully at Dass. "I'm sorry. But that must take secondary place."

"We had a deal. Two weeks for the Hyperspace Chase."

"Dass . . ."

Sky leaned forward. "We're going to Planet X, Rooper. That's the plan you agreed to."

"But with everything . . . The rumors from Jedha— Sky, you don't know everything Fel Ix has said about the Path of the Open Hand and this Leveler and how it affects the Jedi. This is vital. I must speak with my master."

"No." Sky curled their hands into fists. "This is my ship, so we're doing as I say. Come on, Dass." They stood up.

"Stop."

Sky slowly turned with their most arrogant look.

Rooper had stood, as well, and moved past Dass to face Sky. "I know why Dass feels so urgently about finding his ship, and even why Fel Ix wants to go there. But why do you really want to go to Planet X, Sky?"

"I told you before." Sky felt anger hot in their chest. And something else, too, making their pulse beat faster.

"You said glory. Ambition." Rooper crossed her arms. "I don't think that's all of it."

"You don't know me very well then," Sky insisted.

"Your family owns most of the prospectors in the Chase,

at least half! The Grafs will probably get the hyperspace route one way or another. Why does it have to be you?"

"To prove that I can!"

Their words sank into a bright silence as everyone stared at them.

Rooper's expression softened. "I don't believe you. You're more than that."

Sky narrowed their eyes. "Why should I be? Ambition is a good thing to have."

"Some ambition. But not at the loss of—of compassion. Of doing the best thing for the galaxy!"

"I don't care about the galaxy!" Sky cried. "I care about my dad!"

To Sky's horror, they felt tears burning in their eyes. Before any could fall, they turned and fled to the cockpit.

CHAPTER TWENTY

Dass paused only a moment before following Sky.

The Graf pilot was crouched on the deck next to the ancient tech they'd renamed the astro-resonance machine, head down and arms hugging themself. They weren't making any noise. Dass stomped over so Sky knew he was coming and sat, throwing an arm around their back. The two of them stayed that way for a moment, and then slowly Sky leaned into Dass. They sat back on the deck, too, but kept their head down.

"Everyone says he's dead," Sky said, voice muffled by their own arms.

Dass hugged a little tighter, then looked up as Rooper appeared quietly in the hatch.

Sky sighed and sat up. They practically glared at Rooper. But the fight was gone from their voice. "He was on a research trip, looking for Planet X. He'd been looking for a while and was sure he had found a way. Then he just . . . never came back. The family sent out a few messages. Helis did. And my mom. But nothing came back. Nobody knows exactly where he was when his ship vanished. But I heard that planet is beautiful, like a paradise. Everybody knows that." Sky glanced at Dass with hope. "He didn't die in a hyperspace accident or get murdered by Hutts. He made it to Planet X. I know he did. He could still be there, stuck, like your ship is, waiting to be rescued."

Dass winced a little, but when Sky's expression fell, he said, "It's possible. There were a lot of really incredible things there, some dangerous, some not. I . . . it's possible."

"See?" Sky said to Rooper.

The Padawan nodded. She joined them on the deck, on the other side of the machine.

"It's important," Sky added. "Just as important as your Master Silandra is to you."

"Okay," Rooper said.

"Okay?" Sky said breathlessly.

Rooper held out her hand. After a moment, Sky took it. They squeezed each other's hands, then let go.

Just then, the *Brightbird* signaled they were about to drop out of hyperspace.

Dass popped up to take the controls. "No indications of anybody else in this system."

"Great." Sky started situating the astro-resonance machine again, making sure the connections to the navi-computer were in place. "What's your Kessarine doing out there alone?" they asked.

"Cleaning up tea," Rooper said a bit primly.

"Convenient," Sky answered.

Dass set the ship on a clear course and returned to the machine. He took a deep breath as Sky settled the supra-luminite in place. Dass put his hand where it belonged, and Rooper tilted the supraluminite onto its edge. The glow of the connection with the lattice brought back memories of dripping trees and long rainbow ferns, the slow-moving beasts that shimmered violet-blue, the flying fish, all those strange colors, and the smell of the flowers thick as rain.

"It's working," Sky said softly.

Dass smiled, thinking about his dad, about being able to do this, to lead Sky back to their own dad.

He felt a cool hand on his—Rooper's, he assumed—and kept remembering the vivid life of Planet X. Dass held his breath, waiting.

The navicomputer acknowledged the data pouring through the lattice cradle Sky had created.

"Here we go," Sky said. "Got it."

Dass looked up at the viewport as Sky piloted the ship around, then pulled the hyperspace lever. The stars streaked once again into the hyperspace tunnel.

Dass realized pretty quickly after they entered hyperspace that he was really tired. He'd been up for a while, and all the jumping and moving hadn't loaned itself to keeping any kind of good internal clock for the days he'd been on the *Brightbird*. Not to mention he had nearly been eaten by a moon fungus. So Dass took a nap.

When he woke up, he padded out to the galley to find Fel Ix with a small meal he'd put together. It looked like baked bread and protein preserve and a fruit Dass didn't recognize. The Kessarine sat Dass down and told him to eat. It was a little uncomfortable when Dass remembered Fel Ix pressing a blaster to his ribs, but mostly it was easy to give in to the parenting.

"Did Rooper and Sky eat?" he asked around a mouthful of protein.

Fel Ix set down a glass of juice. "They are resting."

"Oh, wow, they just . . . left you alone." Dass wasn't too surprised Rooper would, after she said they were on the same side. But Sky . . .

Fel Ix smiled wryly. "I believe young Sky Graf has locked the ship's controls to their code."

Dass nodded. That sounded more like it. He drank his juice. It tasted acidic, like lompop berries. "Did Sunshine Dobbs give your people the route to the planet?"

The Kessarine blinked his inner and outer eyelids at Dass. Then he said, "I believe so. You were there with him?"

"Yeah, and he's a real slimeball. You shouldn't trust

him. He abandoned me and my dad without a ship or communications because he wanted those routes."

Fel Ix sat down. "I see."

"We heard about what happened on Jedha, you know. The Mother's broadcast went out all across the Outer Rim. She said one of your people was responsible for the destruction. Maybe you shouldn't go back to the Path."

"My children are with the Path," Fel Ix reminded him.

"Oh." Dass frowned.

When Dass finished eating, Fel Ix gathered his dirty dishes despite Dass's protesting. He could do his own recycling!

But then Sky strode in. "We're about to exit hyperspace," they said without preamble. They passed right through the galley, heading for the cockpit.

Rooper wandered in behind them, all put together but stifling a yawn. Dass smiled at her with a little wave.

"Are you hungry, Padawan?" Fel Ix asked.

Rooper seemed a little startled but shook her head. "I want to see where we are. Then I'll eat. Coming, Dass?"

Dass bounced up and followed her. He glanced back at

Fel Ix to invite him along. After a brief hesitation, Fel Ix followed, too.

Sky sat at the pilot station, slowly running a systems check. Dass stepped over the Graf astro-resonance machine, thinking they needed to find a pedestal for it or a cubby or something. Rooper took her spot at the comms station.

"And three, two, *mark*," Sky said, dropping them back out of hyperspace.

The stars snapped to pinpoints again, scattered heavily across the viewport.

Twin planets as small as moons turned around each other: one bright blue with oceans and life, the other dark, stormy, and unfortunately very familiar to Dass.

Oh, no, he thought, his stomach sinking. It had happened again. The machine kept taking them other places he'd been, instead of Planet X, but Dass had never, *ever* wanted to come back here!

It was Gloam.

TWENTY-ONE

"Gloam!" Dass whined.

Rooper's eyes widened at both his tone and the name. This was the place they'd met, trapped together in a huge mine, facing off against big, hairy, winged Katikoots who'd been poisoned and turned into monsters! It was also where Sunshine Dobbs had abandoned Dass and his dad, Spence—they'd nearly died there, and might have if Rooper, Master Silandra, and their Pathfinder team hadn't arrived.

"Gloam?" Sky said. "This isn't Planet X, either. That other planet is civilized. . . ." Sky leaned forward to read the information scrolling down the green-glowing datascreen. "Aubadas. Over three million citizens, a half dozen city centers underground, and a new spaceport. This entry is very recent."

"We know," Dass said morosely. "We've been here."

Sky turned their frown on Dass. "You have? So the machine brought you to a place you know, but not the place we want to be."

"Yeah."

Sky pressed their hands to their face with a groan. "It isn't working. Not how I theorized. What if it's a fake? Or what if it does something I can't figure out because it's so old? What if it's just . . . I don't know, feeding into nothing? Or you're unconsciously prompting the navicomputer. Or consciously." Sky suddenly sat up and glared at Dass.

Dass leapt to his feet. "No, Sky, wait!" His eyes flashed toward Rooper. "We were *here*."

"Yes," Rooper encouraged.

"Sky." Dass grabbed Sky's wrists. "Sky. This was the place Sunshine abandoned me and my dad."

"So? Let's get out of here then," Sky said.

Dass grinned. "No, you don't get it—Sunshine left us here right after we were on Planet X! This was the first place we came out of hyperspace after we left."

"Oh. *Oh*." Sky grinned back, and it expanded into a laugh. "We're close. Maybe even one jump away, if the machine is working."

"I think it's more than one jump. But maybe it had to bring us this way, since it's using me as a key! This is the way I came."

The two of them threw themselves forward to hug each other.

Rooper smiled softly, a little infected by their excitement. But she couldn't share it entirely. This was important to them, but there were other things Rooper needed to be doing. For herself and as a Jedi. She had agreed to join them and didn't regret that. But the situation was changing. She needed to contact Master Silandra and tell her what she'd learned from Fel Ix about the Path and Dalna, and Jedha. Rooper trusted the Force had put her on this journey, that she was where she ought to be—but she couldn't ignore the instinct to go back. It felt urgent. And maybe it had something to do with Fel Ix. Either with keeping him from joining the Path on Planet X or taking him to the Jedi with his vital information. Rooper had been willing to trust him, to a certain extent. Trusting in the Force first let her give him the benefit of the doubt. The Force would bring her new opportunities to contact Master Silandra and get help making the right decision.

Wait. Rooper sat up straighter. When they'd been there before, there had been a comms team behind the Pathfinders, and they'd been setting up a comms buoy network in the area. That meant there was a chance Rooper could reach Batuu!

Suddenly, hope filled her up and she was smiling, too. She turned in the chair and opened a comms channel. The *Brightbird* immediately connected to a local Aubadas buoy. Rooper sent inquiries, and yes! She could send her message directly to Batuu through a complete network of buoys. As long as they remained open, she could be sure her message went through. Rooper keyed in the codes for the Jedi research outpost on Batuu and began: "This is Padawan Rooper Nitani with a message for Jedi Master Silandra Sho, care of the Jedi research outpost at Black Spire, on

Batuu. Master, I am currently on a mission near Aubadas, with Dass Leffbruk and Sky Graf, pilot of the *Brightbird* of planet Thelj. Attaching our identification codes. I have urgent information about the Path of the Open Hand. I will await your response as long as I can. May the Force be with you, Master."

Rooper sent the message and leaned back.

Silence surrounded her. She slowly turned to face Sky and Dass—and Fel Ix, who leaned against the cockpit hatch.

"What are you doing?" Sky demanded.

"I need to get in contact with my master," Rooper answered calmly. Or at least, calmly on the outside. Inside her stomach knotted up. She didn't want to fight.

"But we need to leave."

"Can't we wait just a few hours? Helis can't follow us anymore."

"This is a race, Rooper," Sky insisted. "It's literally called the Hyperspace Chase. We can't just take a break."

"The Path could get to Planet X first," Dass added. "Find my ship first. Fel Ix said they're going."

Rooper looked him right in the eye. "If I can hear from

Master Silandra I'll be more free to continue. I just need to pass on my information at least. Then I can help you wholeheartedly!"

Sky studied her suspiciously. "Why didn't you just put your information in your message then?"

"Please, Sky. Dass." Rooper paused to gather herself. "I don't have parents the way you do. We go to the temple when we are very young, and the Jedi become our family. Master Silandra is not my mother, but you must understand how important to me she is. We're doing this to look for your father, Sky, and your ship, Dass. To prove yourselves to your families. Can't you give me the time to reach Silandra? To know if she is even alive?"

Dass nodded.

Rooper smiled her best encouraging smile, then turned to Sky. "Wouldn't it be good to refuel and make sure everything is ready for whatever comes? Dass said some kind of cloud hides Planet X. That it was difficult and dangerous to fly through?"

"I did," Dass said.

"Then it's better to be fully fueled and maybe even run a diagnostic while we're in a place we can maybe get any parts we need. Besides, Aubadas is friendly to us. It would be polite to say hello."

Sky shook their head. "The *Brightbird* is fine. We have plenty of reserves."

Rooper bit her lip, searching for a more persuasive argument. Fel Ix leaned against the pristine white wall of the corridor leading back to the galley. He hadn't said anything one way or another, keeping out of this argument. But his presence gave her an idea. "Sky. If I manage contact with Master Silandra, it's possible we can leave Fel Ix here instead of dragging him around with us. The Katikoot should be willing to hold him until he can be picked up by the Republic."

Fel Ix frowned. "Rooper," he began.

"Fine," Sky interrupted. "But refuel and a fresh meal only. Then we'll leave no matter what you have or haven't heard from your master." Sky turned back to the pilot's controls. "Where's the spaceport?"

"Ah, they didn't used to have one," Rooper said.

Sky rolled their eyes and muttered something Rooper couldn't hear, but didn't argue when Rooper reached out to the Aubadas capital to ask for permission to land.

CHAPTER TWENTY-TWO

When they settled onto the landing pad, Sky asked Rooper to remain on the ship to watch her prisoner. Rooper agreed, though she disliked thinking of Fel Ix that way. She didn't like thinking about taking any kind of prisoners. Of course it was necessary sometimes, but that didn't make it more pleasant to be controlling somebody's freedom. Even though Fel Ix had tried to steal their ship and had valuable information about the Path.

But Rooper wanted to be there in case any message from Master Silandra arrived. Rooper already worried she wouldn't be able to keep the *Brightbird* in the system long enough for a reply. It was possible Silandra hadn't even been on Batuu to receive Rooper's message. Rooper didn't think she could summon the confidence to convince Sky to wait any longer than the necessary refueling. Dass was clearly not comfortable there, either, despite the ship's not going anywhere near the storm planet Gloam, where he and his dad had been abandoned.

Dass promised to bring Rooper back a sweet snack, though. She was proud of him for venturing off the *Brightbird.* She whispered it to him, and Dass said he wanted to see the glowing river that cut through the cavernous underground city that was the Aubadas capital.

While they waited, Rooper meditated in the center of the galley, cross-legged on the deck. Fel Ix remained, and through the Force Rooper could sense his attention on her. He seemed to want to ask her something. But Rooper didn't want to talk about the Path anymore, or how Jedi supposedly abused the Force. She needed to focus and meditate so she could make the best choices.

Rooper breathed deeply and let herself sink into the brightness of the Force, into its rainbow. She didn't abuse the Force like Fel Ix claimed. She would know. When she touched it, or when she welcomed it to flow through her, that felt good. It was light. If the Force did not want Rooper to connect with it, or use it to sense things or move things or change the galaxy, she simply wouldn't be able to. Maybe if the Path of the Open Hand didn't reject the possibility of using the Force, they would know that, too.

Rooper thought of Master Silandra's shield, and of her own two lightsabers. She imagined the Force inside of her brightening, imagined becoming a shield herself. She could do this. She could listen to the Force and help her friends.

When she finally opened her eyes, feeling surer of herself, Fel Ix had his big golden eyes pinned on her.

Rooper smiled at him, just a little bit. She felt ready.

Fel Ix said, "If you take me to your Jedi Master, it won't matter. I won't tell her anything more than I've told you. I know who I am and who my family is."

"All right," Rooper said.

For a moment the Kessarine just stared back, a little confused maybe. Then he nodded. "All right."

Just then the *Brightbird* chirped that the hold doors had opened. Rooper's comlink beeped, and Dass's voice came through. "We're back. Everything is ready. Are you ready, Rooper?"

"Yes." She considered asking for more time. But she'd trust in the Force. Either her message had gotten through or it hadn't, and either Master Silandra would reach back out or she wouldn't.

Rooper got to her feet so she could greet Sky and Dass when they emerged from the spiral staircase. "It went smoothly?" she asked Sky as a whiff of smoky-smelling air came in along with the Graf.

"And quickly!" Sky grinned, already on their way to the cockpit.

Rooper went after, followed by both Dass and Fel Ix. They took up their usual positions for liftoff. Sky paused to lower a jump seat from the back wall of the cockpit for Fel Ix. The Kessarine took it, positioned behind Rooper at the comms station.

They all buckled in, and as Sky talked with the Aubadas spaceport, Rooper did her best to remain patient and not send another message to Batuu. But it was hard. She bit her bottom lip and centered herself again.

The ship lifted off and quickly gained altitude. It was such a smooth flier, better and sleeker than most of the Jedi shuttles and Republic ships Rooper had been on.

Once they reached the stars, Sky set them on a course that would take them out of the Aubadas gravity well to jump to hyperspace. They spun in their chair and faced Dass. "Let's get that machine going."

With a quick smile, Dass sank to his knees beside the resonator. Rooper took a deep breath and tried not to seem reluctant to join in. They were in this together.

But just then, the comms station chirped with an incoming message.

Rooper's whole body lit up with tension. She reached out slowly and acknowledged.

The message crackled to life from the relay speaker, and relief nearly overwhelmed Rooper as Master Silandra's voice filled the cockpit.

"Padawan, it is good to hear from you. I am glad you are safe and well and with friends."

Though her words were encouraging, Rooper could hear

the concern in them. But Silandra wouldn't take Rooper to task without knowing who else was listening. Even though Rooper definitely deserved it.

"I only just arrived on Batuu to collect you before heading to the Dalnan system. Rok Buran and his new Padawan headed in that direction, chasing after smugglers. There's something wrong with the comms buoys around Dalna, and we're having difficulty reaching him—or anyone. Given the information we have, it's clear that the Path of the Open Hand retreated to their homeworld, and they are gathering ships. It seems likely they are plotting an attack of some kind, such as occurred on Jedha. It is a priority to investigate. Take your ship to Dalna and wait for me there. Do not engage with anything, and keep yourselves hidden until I arrive. And, Rooper, be careful. I trust that you made your choices as wisely as possible, but I am aware of the Graf family and their involvement on Jedha, and it concerns me that your new friend has not been entirely honest with you. Stay safe. May the Force be with you."

The sudden absence of Master Silandra's voice was almost as surprising as its arrival had been.

"I'm not lying," Sky said immediately. "I don't know

anything about Jedha except what I've told you, and I only care about the Hyperspace Chase, and getting to Planet X. Where we're going."

Rooper spared them a glance. "I believe you, Sky. That doesn't mean others of your family are just as honest."

Sky twisted their lips in displeasure. "Like my cousin Tilson, probably." They opened their mouth on a deep breath, then started to say, "But—"

"The Jedi," Fel Ix interrupted. He unbuckled his safety strap and stood. "The Jedi are going to attack my people on Dalna."

Shocked at that interpretation, Rooper stared at the Kessarine. His cheek frills were stiff and almost vibrating. She said, "The Jedi don't attack people. It's an investigation. Master Silandra said it's the Path that is planning another attack—like on Jedha."

Fel Ix said, "Take me back there."

Rooper nodded. She flipped the switch to record a new message, and said, "Acknowledged, Master Silandra. I'll see you on Dalna."

"Rooper!" Sky yelled, leaping to their feet.

Rooper sent her message and turned. She stood up

slowly, trying to seem calm and in charge. She felt this was right. She had to make Sky believe it. "There is so much at stake, Sky."

"My dad—"

Rooper shook her head. "More than that."

"I don't care."

"Then take me back down to Aubadas. I'll find my own way to Dalna without you."

"You can't," Dass said. "I want to stick together."

Rooper tried to remain calm. She was sure of what she needed to do. "Thank you, Dass. I prefer that, too."

"Rooper!" Sky cried. "You agreed. We were in this together. Going to Planet X together."

"I have to follow the Force, Sky. I'm a Jedi. I belong with my master on Dalna. It's the right thing to do."

Sky glanced at Dass, whose eyes were wide. "Dass, tell her."

"I . . . I . . ." he said, looking between Sky and Rooper. "You heard what Master Silandra said, Sky. A lot of lives are at stake, and maybe even your family is involved. If there's something bad about to happen on Dalna, maybe . . ."

Suddenly, Sky moved.

They whirled and slammed a quick series of commands into the pilot station. When they turned back, Sky lifted their chin. "My ship. Locked to my codes. We're going where I say."

Sky tried desperately to stop their hands from shaking. They knew this was their last chance. If they left now, allowed the *Brightbird* to jump to Dalna, that was it. No more opportunities to find Dad, to get to Planet X or find any clues about what happened to him. There could be an escape pod or distress tracker out there, near the paradise planet, anything. Anything.

"Listen to me, Sky," Rooper tried again. "There could be a battle! People could die."

Sky shook their head. "I don't care. People die all the time!"

"Like your father?" Fel Ix said, behind Rooper.

Tension cracked like a calving glacier and Sky's lips pulled back in a grimace. "You can jump out the airlock for all I care about your opinion!"

Rooper stood in front of Fel Ix like a shield. "I think you do care, Sky." She sounded so confident, like she knew exactly who she was and what she was doing.

Sky wondered if that was what it was like to be a Jedi, to always have the Force backing you up. Sky used to feel like they had somebody there for them, always. Dad. But Dad had been gone for more than a year, and even when Helis or their family wanted the same things, it wasn't unconditional support. That was what Rooper radiated right then. That was what Sky wanted to get back. They needed their dad. Sky clenched their jaw and refused to budge. They put their hands against the pilot station. It was theirs. This mission was theirs.

Dass said, "Sky, we should listen to Rooper. We can't just abandon her. She's our friend."

"I thought so," Sky argued. "But apparently not."

The Kessarine put one hand on Rooper's shoulder and curled his fingers there, slowly pushing Rooper aside. He loomed tall but kept that hand on Rooper while watching Sky. The furls on his cheeks were tight with tension. "Sky Graf," he said.

"I have a blaster under this pilot station, and I sure would be happy to stun you," Sky bragged. It sounded too quiet though. Not enough bravado.

Fel Ix inclined his head as if to say, *Go ahead then.* Sky didn't reach for the blaster. Fel Ix said, "How long has your father been missing?"

"Over a year," Sky snapped. It was either that or whisper it and get all teary again.

"I am sorry." Fel Ix stepped closer.

"I don't care."

"I have only been away from my children for a handful of days. Little in comparison."

"So?"

Fel Ix held their gaze. "My children are with the Path of the Open Hand. If the Path is on Dalna, my children are there. If there is a battle there, they could die. My children. Or my partners. Or if we do not return, I could die, or be separated from them by the Jedi. Forever. My children are very small. They will not remember me at all."

"They have—you said they have other parents." Sky knew it was selfish but said it anyway. They clung to their purpose. They had to. Anything else was abandoning Dad. Nobody else was looking for him. Mom, Aunt Jacinda, and even Helis all agreed there was nothing to do. Sky couldn't stand doing nothing.

"Sky!" Dass said, clearly shocked. "You didn't mean that."

Sky ground their teeth again. They did mean it.

Fel Ix said, "Nobody brought your father back to you. Bring me back to my children."

That hit Sky in the gut. They tried to scoff. It came out a little too wet and sad. If somebody had been able to bring Dad home . . .

Dass stepped closer. He didn't reach to touch Sky, and good, because Sky thought if somebody touched them right then, they might burst. "Sky," Dass said softly and urgently. "I get it. My mom died when I was little. I know what it's like to have that pain. That hole there. It's just there, even when you have other people—other parents or family—and you're all working to remake the way you do things. Not to forget, but because of that hole."

Sky shook their head. Their eyes burned, but they widened their lashes and refused to let the tears fall.

"It's awful," Dass whispered. "I get it."

"No, you don't," Sky said thickly, eyes on Fel Ix. The Kessarine watched them back, not seeming angry but . . . sad. Behind him, Rooper looked like she might cry, too.

Sky kept going. "You don't, Dass. You don't get it, because you know what happened to your mom. You know. She died in a shuttle accident. It isn't some huge mystery that's impossible to solve!"

The tears fell then, in straight lines down their cheeks.

Dass said, "I'm sorry. But . . ." He stepped closer again. "Sky, you're right, I know what happened to Mom, but that doesn't make it better. Knowing doesn't bring them back or hurt less."

"You don't know that," Sky whispered. "It would be easier if I knew."

Rooper said, "Sky, the only thing that will make it easier is doing the right thing."

Sky felt their mouth drop open. How could Rooper say something so earnest and so honest? So good?

Sky remembered how excited they'd been to have a real

live Jedi on board, even just a Padawan. How delighted Dad had been all those years earlier when Sky used science to fake Force sensitivity. The stories Dad had told about the Jedi Temple on Coruscant.

And they thought about their mom and aunt. And Helis. What they'd all do in this situation. Shoot the Kessarine and lock the Padawan up if they could manage it. And stick to the plan. Find Dad.

But they hadn't found him. Sky swallowed confusion, anger, pain. The previous year their family had sent ships to look for Dad, and they gave up when there was no sign. Even Helis accepted the reports. It happened, Helis told Sky. People died in space all the time. They couldn't devote more resources to a doomed mission. Then Helis had said, *Come work on this new ship with me.*

The *Brightbird* had been a distraction for Helis. But for Sky it was a promise. They'd use it to keep looking. To find Dad.

"You told me when we first began that you're doing this to prove yourself to your family, because the Grafs are building the frontier," Rooper said. "But what kind of frontier? Doesn't that matter? It does to me, and to Dass. Maybe even to Fel Ix. What are you building?"

Sky couldn't look anywhere but at Rooper then.

"You can help us save other people," Rooper added. "Other people's parents and siblings and children. Right now. We can do it. I know we can. You don't know where your dad is, and I'm so sorry, Sky. But you do know—*we know*—we can help people on Dalna. It's the right thing to do."

"Sky," Dass said. "What would your dad want you to do?"

They broke. Sky's knees gave out, and they leaned back against the pilot's console. For a moment Sky just shut their eyes. Their pulse roared in their ears. With their free hand they pushed their fist against their chest. This was it. It wasn't doing nothing. It was doing the right thing.

"Okay," Sky whispered. "Dass, have the navicomputer find us a route to Dalna."

Fel Ix wished he were with someone who could tell him what to do.

To the Kessarine, a person became an adult when they completed a coming-of-age ritual around the time they turned fifteen years old. Fel Ix had never gone through it himself. He had grown up in a small algae-farming community on the agrarian planet Atalia, with a handful of other Kessarine families. He and his clutch mates had just begun choosing the challenge they would accept for their rituals when Fel Ix met Er Dal. Er Dal was a young Kessarine on his way from Kessar to join his extended family out on the frontier. Er Dal had stopped on Atalia during a layover between transport shuttles and made his way to the Kessarine neighborhood. Er Dal was barely older than Fel Ix, but he'd traveled across a third of the galaxy already. His stories were more exciting than the promise of farming Fel Ix had grown up with, and when Er Dal caught his next transport, Fel Ix ran away with him.

A couple of adventures and meandering months later, they met Ferize on a different transport. She was traveling with a handful of the Path of the Open Hand. The Path welcomed Fel Ix and Er Dal, fed them, and offered them a reason to trust in the galaxy: the Force. Fel Ix believed that the Force itself had brought him to Er Dal and Ferize. And the Force had given them all to the Path. The three Kessarine made their nest together in the palm of that generous hand.

The Path was good. Fel Ix believed that. The Path was his family. The Path believed in using the strengths of its members to continue the work of helping the galaxy understand that the only way to live with the Force was in harmony, with clarity, and for freedom.

Only, Fel Ix wasn't with them now. He didn't know how to be without family.

He'd gone directly from his own childhood clutch, to partners, to the Path. He'd never been truly on his own.

The Mother had given him a mission: to infiltrate certain comms buoys with the unique code she'd acquired. The Force itself made its will clear to the Mother; so following her was following the Force. Fel Ix's friend Marda Ro followed the Mother, too. Fel Ix wanted Marda to be happy with his service, and to make the Mother proud. He wanted them to tell him what to do.

But they weren't there.

Fel Ix did not want to question his loyalty. Even if his conversations with Rooper suggested the Path might not be the only way, it remained *his* way. Yet he couldn't help wondering whether focusing on the comms buoys, his original mission, still mattered more than working with these children. He had boarded the *Brightbird* because of the Padawan, because the Mother wanted him on the lookout for Jedi. He followed what he'd believed to be the will of the Force. It had brought him to Rooper Nitani. Maybe he was making a difference for the Force. But maybe he was mistaken and needed to get back. For a while he thought allowing them to take him on their journey to Planet X would reunite him with the Path, or he would find a time to slip away from the overly kind Jedi Padawan. He had access to a Path credit stream for emergencies. But if neither Planet X nor escaping was possible, what did he need to do?

As the *Brightbird* flew through hyperspace toward Dalna, Fel Ix sat himself in the galley with a simple cup of the very nice tea he'd found. He wished he could relax his tails and give them a good stretch. Kessarine did not need as much sleep as many sentient beings, and he'd found that if he slowed his thoughts and meditated on the Force as was taught by the Path, he could achieve a state of peace that allowed him to both think through problems and emerge refreshed.

He needed that peace. He needed to figure out his next step on his own.

Returning to Dalna was not something he'd expected. When the Path had boarded the *Gaze Electric*, the Mother implied that they were leaving Dalna forever. They would traverse the stars, spreading the harmony, clarity, and freedom of the Open Hand. Despite the new edge of urgency Fel Ix and his partners sensed in not only their friend Marda but in the leadership of the Path, Fel Ix had trusted in the way of the Path. Trusted that the Mother knew the will of the Force.

"You're good at that," Rooper said.

Fel Ix opened his eyes. They were drier than he liked. But he had none of the thick drops Ferize kept in their nest. "At?"

The young Jedi slid into the booth beside him. "Communing with the Force."

"All who join the Path of the Open Hand are fluent in meditation."

Rooper hummed. "Tell me about Dalna."

Fel Ix studied her. She folded her hands together on the galley table, holding his gaze. She reminded him of Marda sometimes: Rooper was good, was eager to please, and tried to behave older than her actual age. "Dalna is a small planet circling two suns. There are volcanoes and river valleys. Not very many people live there."

"And the Path?"

"Has taken to the stars. There is no reason for us to return to Dalna."

Rooper frowned. "Then why would the Mother take you back there?"

"It is not for me to question her wisdom. The Force

gives her insight, and she follows that. You should consider that the Mother knows the Force as well as any living being. Perhaps better."

"Can any single person know the Force best?" Rooper asked.

Fel Ix flipped one long-fingered hand in a slight shrug.

Rooper reached her hand toward the small pot of tea gone cold at Fel Ix's elbow. The pale green pot lifted off the table, tugged by invisible strings.

Fel Ix swallowed. He tried not to appear anxious at the display of Force abuse. The Jedi drew the teapot to herself and poured a sip into one of the empty cups on the tray. She was not showing off; Fel Ix understood that. Rooper wanted to remind him that she did not believe the Path's philosophy was valid.

"Can you think of any reason the Mother would return to Dalna? It's already a war zone, sharing a sector with Eiram and E'ronoh."

Fel Ix knew little about the twin planets that had been warring for as long as he'd been on the frontier. There had been numerous peace treaties, but none had stuck. The most recent treaty had broken down only days earlier on Jedha.

He said, "Dalna was our home for many years. Perhaps she wants to allow us all to rest after what happened on Jedha." Fel Ix did not believe it: the Mother was passionate about her mission in the stars. That was why she'd sent him after the comms buoys, why she needed more Levelers from Planet X.

"Would she bring the dangers of the battle at Jedha to a place she thought of as her home?" Rooper asked.

Fel Ix opened his mouth to deny it but stopped. The Mother would do whatever she believed the Force wanted her to do. Members of the Path had died in the past, on missions from the Mother. It was always a possibility, to die for the Path.

"I don't know," Fel Ix said.

"Do you know what the Mother wants?"

"For the Force to be free," he answered easily.

But as he spoke, Fel Ix realized there was something that *he* wanted even more than he wanted the Force to be free. What Fel Ix wanted most was to return to his partners and hatchlings.

And it was possible the best way to do that was by helping this Jedi.

CHAPTER TWENTY-FIVE

The *Brightbird* emerged in the Dalnan system after a quiet hyperspace flight.

Sky was pretty angry about it.

Despite choosing to help Rooper return to her master, Sky's whole heart still screamed to be heading out on the next leg of their journey to Planet X. This compromise was what they got for being part of a team. Teamwork. Needing other people. That wasn't the Graf way for a reason.

Grafs were supposed to get what they wanted. Make it, buy it, steal it. Just get it. Teams were meant to be hired, not collected like friends. Hired teams could be left behind or disbanded, and hired teams just did what they were told. They didn't convince you that what you wanted was selfish. They didn't make you do the right thing.

But Sky knew Dass was right. Their dad would want Sky to help the Jedi. To be good.

Maybe if Sky tried to find a reason that doing the right thing wasn't just good but also aligned with the Graf way, it would help. Maybe the wild rancor chase to Planet X wasn't the most lucrative option, even if they could find Dad. It was dangerous, and taking up all Sky's resources. Maybe the long-term benefits of helping Rooper at Dalna would get them more. A Jedi ally. Inroads into the conflict-riddled sectors of Dalna and Eiram and E'ronoh. There was always money to be made in war. Though the thought made Sky queasy.

Sky did wonder if the trouble with communications Silandra Sho had mentioned was more due to Dalna's being a war zone than to the Path of the Open Hand. On the other hand, Silandra Sho had also said Grafs were involved in the mess on Jedha, so it was possible their family was already up to their necks in this.

Well. Sky would find out! And use it to their advantage.

The ship slipped into realspace far enough from Dalna not to be noticed right away, giving them a chance to scan the planet and any ships in orbit before they likely paid much attention in return.

All four of the *Brightbird*'s passengers crowded around the viewport.

The blue-and-green planet hung prettily against the stars, unthreatening.

But surrounding it were dozens of ships. Sky's mouth dropped open. The *Brightbird* rang out with proximity alerts concerning the ramshackle navy enveloping Dalna. Sky's eyes, however, went straight to the largest of the ships: a long, dangerous-looking battleship in orbit over one of the northern continents.

Dass stepped closer to the viewport. "I know that ship." He pointed toward one of the junkier-looking little transports off starboard. "It's captained by a prospector named Alala Ninbiri, and Dad always steered clear of them. They smuggled sometimes."

"That one," Sky said, nodding with their chin to a different transport, "looks like it has one of those Hutt engine mods."

"Sky," Rooper said, tightening her grip on Sky's shoulder. The Padawan was staring at the long, scary-looking cruiser.

"It's the *Gaze Electric*," Fel Ix murmured.

"Ping the buoy," Rooper said. "Let's get to work, see if we can find Master Rok."

At the comms station, Sky nodded. "This buoy is really unsteady," they said.

Dass stood next to the pilot's chair, watching the clusters of haphazard ships as the *Brightbird* drew nearer to Dalna. "Do you know which one is Master Silandra's ship?" he asked.

"No, but it's likely she'll be on a Republic transport," Rooper answered. "Look for something that resembles a Pathfinder ship. And Master Buran will have something like that, too, since he's with a Pathfinder team right now."

"Have you seen him since Aubadas?"

Rooper shook her head. "No. I hope he's doing well. He lost his first Padawan, and we're supposed to be good at letting distress like that move into the Force, but it's hard."

"What are all these ships doing here?" Dass said. "At

least some of them should be in the Chase with us. Why would they come to Dalna?"

"Money," Sky said darkly. "Somebody offered them more money than they could win through the Hyperspace Chase."

"The Mother has money," Rooper said. "In that announcement I read, she promised a lot of financial aid to the Convocation after Jedha."

Fel Ix sucked in a sharp breath.

"Can you send out a call for Jedi Rok Buran?" Rooper asked as she leaned over Sky.

Sky looked at her over their shoulder. "Feel free," they said, shifting back to the pilot's station. Rooper slid into the comms chair.

Dass said, "Maybe don't project to everyone you're a Jedi looking for another Jedi? If this is really as messy as everybody thinks, we don't want to draw attention."

"Just use an open call," Sky suggested.

Rooper agreed. After flicking the switch, she keyed in the right frequency and said, "Rooper Nitani, looking for Rok Buran. Rok, are you here? This is Rooper Nitani. We are near orbit at Dalna. Are you here?" Rooper requested the ship to send her message on a loop via ship-to-ship comms. If Rok was in the system, he should be able to receive it.

The *Brightbird* drifted nearer and nearer to the planet. As they approached, the great battleship controlled by the Path of the Open Hand curled into view. The distant twin suns at the heart of the system glinted off its nose and then glittered off the viewports along its sharklike length.

"When I left them," Fel Ix said, "they were on that ship. The *Gaze Electric*."

Sky stared out at it. It would be extremely risky to hail them, to find out about Fel Ix's family.

"Hang back, Sky," Rooper said. "We don't want trouble."

"Are we still in contact with the buoy?" Sky asked instead of acknowledging what she'd said. "It was unstable, and I couldn't hold down a signal."

"I'll try."

Sky glanced over and saw Rooper make an attempt. Then another. Frowning, Rooper said, "The buoy is there, obviously, but it's like the *Brightbird*'s signals just slip around it instead of locking into the right frequencies."

"So we only have ship-to-ship communications for

now," Dass said. "Can you . . . reach out with the Force and find Silandra?"

Rooper winced. "I might be able to. I know her well enough. If she's near. But I definitely can't speak with her that way."

Standing tensely near the exit hatch, Fel Ix said, "The Path likely has control of the buoy."

Sudden understanding nearly made Sky laugh. They might have, if their realization weren't so bad. Sky said, "You weren't fixing the buoy when we found you. You were sabotaging it!"

Rooper spun in the comms chair to stare at Fel Ix. "How many buoys? How much does the Path control?"

Fel Ix shook his head. "I do not know. I was interrupted in my mission, and likely not the only team with a network map."

"What was the point of your mission, exactly?" Sky asked.

Fel Ix kept his mouth shut.

"Come on, tell us. You want our help getting back to your family, you help us now."

Rooper added, "This is the best way to ensure people

aren't harmed. Communications matter. The Jedi have to be able to talk to the Path, or to the Republic and all these other ships."

"Call for help," Dass said.

"I want my family safe," Fel Ix insisted.

"I give you my word I'll do whatever I can to reunite you with them, Fel Ix," Rooper said. "The Jedi would never harm noncombatants—we try not to harm anybody."

"Try."

"That's all any of us are doing, Fel Ix. Ending this conflict sooner is the best way to make sure your family survives. If the Jedi can communicate, we will do everything we can not to fight."

Fel Ix said, "I do not know specifics that might help. The Mother obeys the will of the Force. Her goals are its goals."

Frustrated, Sky considered threatening the Kessarine with the airlock again, but Rooper said, "Fel Ix. I trust the Force, too. I listen to it as best I can. All Jedi do. A conflict between the Path and the Jedi isn't inevitable! Not if we talk to each other."

Just then the comms station crackled, and a rough

voice came through: "Rooper Nitani, Rok here. I'm near your position. Good to hear from you."

Rooper grabbed the speaker and pressed the activation switch. "Master Buran! I'm so glad to hear from you, too. Master Silandra let me know she couldn't reach you. She's on her way. Do you require any aid?"

Sky leapt into Rooper's space and hit a few buttons. "Get on a closed channel, Rooper."

"Silandra isn't with you?" The frown was apparent in Rok Buran's voice. "Who is that then?"

"No—no, but she's supposed to meet me here. I'm in the *Brightbird*. Did you get the ID code?"

"My Padawan Coron grabbed it. We're in a disguised Republic transport. What we really need is to get the communications back up. Ship-to-ship comms are working at close range, but I'm having trouble with the buoy and subspace relays. We need to reach any Jedi on Dalna."

"I think we can get the buoy functioning properly again," Rooper said.

"You have a comms team with you?"

"No, but we can do it anyway," she said, turning enough to eye Fel Ix.

"The sooner the better, Rooper."

"Yes, Master Buran."

Rooper looked to Sky, who nodded in agreement. They could definitely fix the buoys with the right opportunity. Knowing what Fel Ix had done would make it a lot easier, though.

Rooper said to Fel Ix. "We can figure it out without you, but if you help us it will go a long way with the Republic."

"I do not need to be indebted to the Jedi."

"That isn't—"

"Uh, friends?" Dass said. They looked at him, where he was in the pilot seat. "Do it because we're friends?"

"Oh, poodoo," Sky muttered, spinning around. Their hands flew over the controls. "I can figure it out myself."

"Fel Ix," Rooper said. "The Force brought us together. We don't have to be at war. The Force is part of us all."

The Kessarine's gaze shot up to meet Rooper's.

She said, "We're here for a reason. Make that reason a good one. Make your family proud."

While Fel Ix stared at Rooper, Sky thought about how it was both nice and annoying for Rooper to turn her ace persuasion skills on somebody other than Sky for once.

Finally, Fel Ix blinked his inner eyelids. "I need a few minutes once I have my hands on the buoy," he said. "And I only know how to remove the data I inserted, not how to make sure it's fully functioning again."

"Between the two of us, we can manage," Sky said. Their pulse picked up at the prospect of immediate action.

"Good," Rooper said. "Once we reach the buoy and start interfering, though, everybody will be on us. Including the Mother's battleship."

"We'll be easy targets, even with somebody in the cannon nest," Sky said.

"No," Rooper said. "We don't need to hurt anybody."

Dass leapt to his feet. "Wait!" he said breathlessly. "I have a plan!"

TWENTY-SIX

Dass vibrated with excitement—and nerves. His hands sweated a little as he readied his part in the plan. It was a really big part.

But he could do it.

Next to him, Rooper squeezed his shoulder. She was at the navicomputer, which was calculating a fast jump that should last only a few minutes—barely taking them out of the system. "It's almost ready," she said.

"We're in position," Sky said over the comm. They were down in the hold with Fel Ix, ready at the airlock.

"Got the route," Rooper said. "When we have the buoy,

we'll need a fast burn for just over a minute to get clear of everything and jump."

"Okay," Dass said. "Okay."

He didn't mark go. He stared at the lights on the pilot's console. He swallowed. He could do this.

"The Force is with you," Rooper murmured. "We can do this."

"Rooper!" Sky snapped through the comms. "Get down here and get suited up."

"I've got this," Dass said, hoping he sounded more confident than he felt.

Rooper ran out of the cockpit.

While he waited to hear they were ready in the cargo hold, Dass called up the holomap. It flashed to blue life in front of the viewport. Enemy ships were marked in green, and the buoy was bright red. Rooper and Dass had plotted a course through the ships to the buoy, and then a direct route out to the hyperspace jump point. They'd take the buoy on a fast jump closer to Eiram and E'ronoh, where they could repair it in peace.

But first they had to borrow it.

The comm crackled. "We're ready down here," Sky said.

"Okay, Sky, I'm making the approach." Dass let out a long breath, and then he pulled the yoke. The *Brightbird* shot forward fast.

Dass focused and pulled up, turning the *Brightbird* over to slip between two merc ships, then taking a direct course toward the buoy. The *Brightbird* compensated for the sharp turn, dodging around the transports and hopefully confusing anybody paying attention.

"Get ready, Sky. In twenty!" Dass pushed the *Brightbird* as fast as he could in such close quarters, trying to ignore the looming battleship that was definitely near enough to blast them out of the sky.

They barely skimmed around a bulbous prospecting ship—so close Dass could see the other pilot! Another ship shifted out of their way, and Dass had the urge to wave as they blasted past. They were almost there. "Ten!"

A laser shot across their bow, and Dass dove, then pulled up and aimed again. He increased their speed.

The *Brightbird* overshot the comms buoy, and Dass said, "Open the airlock!"

He couldn't hear any response. Sweat tracked down

his nose. Dass threw the ship into reverse and swung it around. His gaze was locked on the bright red buoy target on the grid, his breath coming hard.

"Open and ready to catch!" Sky yelled through the comms.

The *Brightbird* backed up so fast it was almost like it was being yanked.

※

Down in the hold, Rooper focused her awareness through the Force. The star field she could see out the gaping open hold doors glimmered with rainbows of color. And there was the comms buoy, fast approaching.

She, Sky, and Fel Ix all wore fancy Graf-designed space suits and were tethered to safety rings inside the *Brightbird*. Dass twisted the ship so the bay doors matched up their trajectory with the tilt of the buoy. It was Rooper's job to steady the buoy after Fel Ix shot a magnetic rope at it to drag it in.

Sky and Fel Ix joined Rooper at the open bay door, their suits lit up with bright blue and white, indicating the life support and the active boots specially designed, Sky had explained, to link with the alloy of the *Brightbird*. Fel Ix aimed the compressor that held the mag-rope.

The buoy zipped toward them, closer, closer, and then Sky said, "Go!"

The *Brightbird* came to nearly a complete stop and tilted down. The hold drifted up, like a mouth ready to swallow up the buoy, and for a second they were just floating in space.

"Now," Sky said to Fel Ix. He steadied his legs and fired.

The Kessarine's aim was perfect. The magnet hit the buoy on its narrow ring, and the rope—made of the same duraline as their safety harnesses—snapped into place.

Rooper reached one hand out to focus the Force better. She kept her eyes open wide while Fel Ix and Sky dragged on the rope, pulling the buoy closer. Rooper breathed slowly through pursed lips and used the Force to hold the buoy steady. If she let it tilt the wrong way, the long antennas on the bottom would break off when the hold swallowed it up.

"Rooper!" Dass cried through the comms. His voice rang inside the helmet she wore. "One of the mercs! Planetside!"

Rooper glanced toward Dalna just in time to see an enemy ship aiming its nose at them.

Without thinking, Rooper pushed off the bay door. She darted into open space, trusting the safety harness would hold. "Get the buoy," she said, releasing her focus on the Force.

The other ship fired.

Rooper had both lightsabers out in an instant, crossed in front of her. She screamed with the effort of concentrating as the blaster fire slammed into her crossed sabers. The vivid blue light was blinding, and Rooper was thrown back by the impact. She let the momentum toss her heels over her head and concentrated on controlling the spin. Three spins and Rooper slowed to a stop right side up.

They fired again, and again. Rooper gritted her teeth and shielded her friends. The Force blazed up her arms, and her lightsabers seemed to spark even in the nothingness of space. Each bolt she caught flung her back—she let the energy move her and bent her knees as she hit the hull of the *Brightbird*, then pushed herself off to meet another. She spun and met each shot just in time. The blaster fire ricocheted back toward the other ship, angling off into space.

Everybody was yelling in her comms.

"—back in! Get her, too!" Sky was crying.

"Don't bank hard," Fel Ix said.

Dass yelled Rooper's name over and over.

"I'm all right," she whispered just as the tug on her safety tether dragged her body backward. Rooper's arms felt like noodles, and her ears rang.

"We've almost got her."

Rooper remembered belatedly to shut off her light-sabers, but kept them in her hands. She wasn't sure she could let them go even to sheathe them right then. Her bones seemed like they still were vibrating.

An arm circled around her waist, and suddenly her boots snapped down to connect with the inside of the *Brightbird*'s bay.

"Got her!" screamed Sky. "Closing the bay! Get us out of here, Dass."

❧

Up in the cockpit, the comms station shrieked with different ships all trying to get their attention at once. Alerts blared.

Dass let his mouth widen into a panicked grin. That ship that had shot at them came around with cannons hot. "Shields up!"

The ship's shield array crackled into place just in time. The *Brightbird* shuddered through a hit. Then Dass angled down and spiraled around another enemy transport. "Just a minute until we're at the hyperspace mark! Hold on!"

Dass felt lightheaded but leaned into the speed. Distantly he realized he heard Helis Graf's voice again through the cacophony of comm channels, but he ignored it. There, there was the mark.

"Jumping!" he warned, and reached over to hit the lever. The whole ship leapt forward between one second and the next.

The stars streaked in the viewport and Dass let go of the controls with a huge gasp of air.

TWENTY-SEVEN

The moment the hold doors slid shut, Sky unhooked the helmet of their space suit and threw it back from their face, then unlatched the duraline harness around their chest. "Rooper," they said, scrambling to the Padawan, who was collapsed in Fel Ix's lap.

Sky grabbed Rooper's helmet, too, unhooking the latches. Rooper's eyes were tightly shut, but when the helmet hissed free, Rooper said, "Sky. Did we get it?"

Sky looked toward the comms buoy rocking hard on its side at the far end of the hold. A long scratch marred the formerly pristine deck of the *Brightbird*, and Sky tried not to care. Their pulse pounded in their skull. That was a shockingly dangerous plan, but Dass had flown great. And Rooper had held off a ship's cannon with only her lightsabers and the Force.

"We got it," Fel Ix said. He gently helped Rooper up.

"Shield's up!" Dass's voice blared through the comms.

The ship jolted like they'd been hit with something, and then Sky heard yelling that echoed dully through the ceiling. Before Sky had a chance to really worry, they felt the telltale shudder of a jump to hyperspace.

Sky knelt there for a second to catch their breath. Nothing bad happened. The ship thrummed with power. They were fine. Rooper reached out and grabbed their hand. Sky squeezed back.

Glancing over at Fel Ix, they saw the Kessarine unlocking his helmet.

"I'll go check on Dass," Rooper said.

"You good?"

Rooper nodded, but it took a moment for her to free herself from the duraline harness. Then she stumbled across the metal threshold into the stairwell. Rooper paused on the first step and smiled tiredly at Sky over her shoulder before she climbed up and vanished.

"Let's get this done," Sky said to Fel Ix.

The buoy glittered with a half dozen lights. It was about twice as long as Sky was tall, from the dishes on its dome to the longest of the underside piers. Sky took in as much as they could. The buoy had little thrusters to keep it in the right position, and several self-sustaining solar batteries. The brains of the thing weren't as sophisticated as a droid's, and it didn't have any personality, but it was complex. It had to hold tons of algorithms and data bundles constantly.

Fel Ix knelt on the other side of the buoy and reached to access a dataport. Sky hurried to join him.

The Kessarine started by popping a narrow hatch on the surface. Sky dug a data plug out of their jumpsuit pocket and inserted it. They initiated a diagnostic. But as Fel Ix keyed in a few commands and the codes transmitted to Sky's datapad, Sky stopped in shock.

"These are . . ." They lifted their gaze to Fel Ix's big golden eyes.

"What? We need to recalibrate the code or use a replacement."

"It's . . . Graffian." Sky swallowed their surprise. "This tech is . . . Graf. The codes. Look." Sky pointed at a few of the figures on the screen. It was a shared written language the Grafs were still developing for interfamily communications.

Fel Ix hummed. "Those are the symbols I had to memorize. I was told they had no external meaning, but only worked with these access codes."

"How do you—how does the Path have Graf codes? These characters are supposed to be only for us. They're private."

Fel Ix frowned. "Does that matter right now?"

Sky paused with their mouth open. It meant Sky could definitely fix this whole buoy. Not only strip out all the damaging codes the Path had inserted but reprogram it to work exactly the way it should. They could erase all traces of anything wrong with it. But . . . should they?

The Grafs must have sold this technology to the Path of the Open Hand. For Sky, undoing that would be openly going against their own family. That wasn't just leaving Dad lost or dead; that was betrayal.

Sky's mouth was dry.

Fel Ix blinked both inner and outer eyelids, then got to work.

Sky sat back on their heels. What should they do? Just stand by and be able to say they hadn't participated?

No. It was just as bad to do nothing. The only choices were to stop Fel Ix and return the Graf-infected buoy or to wipe the Graf tech.

Wait. That wasn't all they could do.

Sky could quickly reprogram a datacard with their own algorithms, and it would talk to the whole network of buoys infected with Graffian code. This buoy would be able to send out a burst of data—just like the data bundle with their hyperspace routes that Helis had coded the *Brightbird*'s navicomputer to drop so he could track them. But this data burst would be sent out to any buoys in this one's network, rewriting the malware to make it inert.

That sure would make a statement to Sky's family. Even if it ruined their alliance or whatever they had going with the Path of the Open Hand, Sky's name would rush through the Graf cousin comms like a virus. Not for being a crybaby or for undermining their plan, but for besting them.

If Sky was going to go against their family in this, at least they could do it with ambition and style. Their own kind of style.

Maybe even Rooper would admire it.

Determined, Sky got to work.

TWENTY-EIGHT

The *Brightbird* dropped back into Dalnan space, and Dass didn't hesitate as he aimed the ship right into the fray.

Rooper gripped his shoulder tightly in reassurance for both of them, then moved to the rear of the cockpit and hit the control to lower the lift that would take her up to the cannon nest. It hissed down. She didn't want to use the cannon as a threat, but she was exhausted from her extreme channeling of the Force just moments earlier. This was the tool she could use right now. It would be all right. She didn't really think she'd need it anyway.

Rooper activated the comm. "Sky, I'm getting in the nest, just in case. It's five minutes to release of the buoy, as long as nothing interferes."

"Roger, Rooper—we're ready down here. Locked in and waiting for Dass's cue to open the doors."

Rooper climbed into the lift and sent it up as Dass said, "I'll swing around, and the momentum should launch it as long as you two position it at the edge."

The lift locked Rooper out of the cockpit. She climbed forward into the cannon nest.

"Will do," Sky said.

It took only a moment for Rooper to position herself in the chair and lower the cannon interface. It surrounded her head and shoulders like a basket. Despite having used it once before, Rooper reminded herself where the targeting system and various triggers were before starting it up. A glowing grid appeared, similar to the one Dass had used on the viewport for his trick maneuvering.

"Incoming!" Dass called. "One minute to launch!"

The grid flared with ships moving into their immediate space, and Rooper put both hands on the cannon controls. There were actually three cannons controlled by this nest. All ready and full up. Rooper waited. She didn't want to shoot anybody.

One ship pulled in to intercept course, and the *Brightbird* dodged smoothly. Dass was an excellent pilot, Rooper thought. She hoped he would pursue it.

She centered herself, letting her awareness open to the targeting system and the ship itself, feeling the Force flow. Despite her weariness, the Force was just as lively and bright as always. The Force was infinite. And it was the Force, and her instincts, she would rely on to know if she needed to shoot.

Dass pushed the ship fast. Rooper could hear the engines whine, but nothing else. One of the ships shot at them, but Rooper didn't return fire: the shields managed it.

"Dropping shields in ten!" Dass called. "Rooper, cover us!"

Her fingers flew as she called up a pattern for suppressing fire—not targeted to hit anybody.

"Ready!" Sky called. "Hangar open!"

The ship twisted, and Rooper opened fire.

The *Brightbird* lit up as the three cannons fired bright red lasers, scattering the shots to force other ships back.

"Hang on!" Dass yelled, and the ship arced suddenly, slowing down to fling the buoy out.

"The buoy is off!" Sky screamed. "Closing—up!"

Rooper sent out another round of suppressive shots, breathing carefully.

"Shields back up. I'm getting us out of here," Dass said.

"Did the buoy land right?" Rooper asked, pulling back on the cannons.

The ship lurched as a few of the enemy ships chased them. Rooper watched them through the targeting system. She wished she had a real viewport.

"It's settling its thrusters," Sky called through the comms. "Close to the same spot, within the correct range!"

"Good," Rooper said, trying to sound calm. "Dass?"

"Some people on our tail."

"I'm heading up," Sky said.

Rooper stayed put. Before she'd gone up there, she'd started the navicomputer calculating an escape jump. They just needed to get far enough away from whatever was happening on Dalna. "Sky, when you get there, patch the comms up to me?"

"Yep!" Sky said. "Just a minute."

"Rooper, that transport behind us is powering up something!" Dass said, voice tight. "I can't get us away any faster. You have to fire!"

Rooper reached out to touch the offending dot that represented the close ship and focused. She took a deep breath, then let it hiss out slowly through her teeth as she pulled the trigger.

The cannon system pinged and showed her hits to the other ship's shields. They returned fire.

"Comms are yours!" she heard Sky say.

Rooper shot at the other ship again, even as the *Brightbird* dodged and turned. Her shot was interrupted by another ship. It looked like a wild mess out there, and fortunately a lot of the ships were ignoring the *Brightbird*.

Taking advantage of the temporary lack of fire, Rooper flicked on the comm. "Master Buran! It's Rooper—are you there?"

"Here, Rooper. Catching up to you for cover in a minute!"

"Is the buoy working? Can you reach anyone?"

"Stand by. . . ."

A moment passed. The *Brightbird* angled hard and

twisted again. Rooper was tossed onto her shoulder. Then Master Buran said, "Rooper, you did it! We've got contact!"

Relief washed through her. "Great. Since we obviously borrowed the buoy, any cover we might have had is blown. We have to get out of here, Master. Silandra is still coming to meet me. Can you tell her I'll contact her again and that I'm okay?"

"I can. Be careful, Rooper. May—"

The ship shuddered with a hard hit to their shields. Rooper studied the targeting grid in panic, searching for the right place to shoot back.

But another ship entered their space, right behind them and moving fast.

"This one is just as fast as us!" Dass yelled. "And gaining! Fire, Rooper!"

Before she could, the other ship opened fire! But the shots passed the *Brightbird*, and one of the smuggler transports behind them exploded.

"What's going on out there?" Rooper demanded.

Sky yelled, "It's my brother!"

CHAPTER TWENTY-NINE

Sky panted as they leaned over Dass. Every fiber of their body wanted to take over piloting, but Dass was doing great, and there wasn't time.

Helis's ship caught up with them, flanking the *Brightbird*, and continued to shoot at the other ships chasing them. They were so close to being free of Dalna and able to jump, but Helis was getting in the way!

Sky leaned over and slammed on the ship-to-ship comms. "Helis, back off! We have to get out of here!"

"Stop right there, Sky! Just surrender to me. You've

caused enough trouble. I'm almost close enough to knock out your shields."

"I can't believe you're working with the Path."

"I'm not working with anybody," Helis sneered. "Unless you count Precoria San Tekka and the Hyperspace Chase. I don't even want to be in this system."

Dass caught Sky's eye and lifted his eyebrows. Sky nodded with a grim smile and glanced at the navicomputer.

Taking the hint, Dass checked it, then gave Sky a thumbs-up before flashing four fingers. Okay, four minutes to jump. If Sky could keep Helis talking while they both moved out of the Dalnan system, Helis wouldn't fire until it was too late.

Sky said, "Helis, it's Graf tech that was sabotaging the comms buoy here, Graf tech the Path of the Open Hand has been using to upset comms networks all over the Outer Rim."

"And you disrupted it?" Helis sounded appalled. "I saw your little stunt."

"Sky," Dass said softly and intensely, "I think he's trying to break in again."

"Stay off my ship, Helis!" Sky snapped.

"My ship, Sky, and if you know what's good for you, you'd better stop interfering here!"

"Tell me what's going on with the Path! I thought they're the ones who broke into the compound on Thelj!"

Helis paused. Sky looked pointedly back at Fel Ix, in the jump seat. The Kessarine shrugged.

Helis said, "I don't know anything about us selling anything to the Path, or working with them, but you shouldn't be surprised, kid. We work with everybody who has enough credits."

"A dangerous way to work."

"Tilson is dead, so you're probably right."

"What!" Sky cried before they could stop themself. Their cousin Tilson was known for taking bad deals for a certain price. Sky didn't like him at all, but he was still a Graf and they didn't want him dead.

Helis said, "He died on Jedha. I just found out. Unclear how or why, but the Path of the Open Hand was involved. Aunt Jacinda redirected me here to inquire with them. But I didn't expect to find you here! It's too dangerous, Sky."

Sky felt queasy at all this new information. They didn't want Helis in danger. They couldn't lose him, too.

"Tell me where you're—"

The *Brightbird* shuddered.

"We're hit," Dass said.

"Helis!" Sky yelled at their brother.

"Stop running from me, Sky!"

Sky cut out the ship-to-ship comms and switched to *Brightbird* intercom only. "Rooper, fire back!"

"That's your brother!"

"You probably can't hurt him anyway. We just need . . . how long, Dass?"

"One minute."

"One minute, Rooper! Then we'll jump."

Rooper didn't answer, but the ship showed their cannons shifting and aiming at Helis.

Sky, who was staring out the viewport, noticed the second a big ship flashed out of hyperspace, dead ahead of them.

Immediately, the *Brightbird*'s alerts blared.

"Changing course," Dass said. "Two more minutes."

They lurched up, and the stars spiraled as Dass put them into a corkscrew.

Sky tapped some commands. The ship that had appeared was about three times bigger than the *Brightbird*, and with Republic codes. Hopefully they were just joining the mess on Dalna and would ignore the *Brightbird*, Sky thought.

Suddenly, the cockpit was filled with another voice. "*Brightbird*, acknowledge. Transmitting navigational route. Confirm receipt and let me know you are well, Rooper."

"Incoming data," Dass said as Sky leaned in to transfer.

"Master Silandra!" Rooper cried. "That's her, Sky! Send back!"

Sky hit the switch. "This is the *Brightbird*. Rooper says hi."

Before the Jedi Master could respond, Helis broke through again. Ship-to-ship comms were so annoyingly open.

"This is Helis Graf of the *Starlily*, and the *Brightbird* belongs to me. Any attempt to escort it away will be considered hostile."

Sky's mouth fell open in shock.

But Master Silandra answered very coolly, "Mr. Graf, I am Silandra Sho of the Jedi. You are welcome to accompany us out of the system, but the *Brightbird* is coming with me. Now."

"New coordinates are incoming," Dass said.

The lift from the cannon nest hissed as it lowered, and Rooper nearly fell out. "Do what she says," Rooper urged.

Distantly, Sky was aware of Helis arguing with Rooper's master, but Sky could only panic. It was a low-grade panic, deep and vibrating. They didn't know what to do. If they left with Master Silandra, who knew what Helis would report. This was such a mess. Sky really wished they were out in hyperspace, still trying to find their dad. But how could they resist this firepower *and* Helis, especially when Rooper didn't want to resist.

Rooper took Sky's shoulders in her hands. "Sky," she said. Supportive. Intense.

Behind them, Dass said, "I need to make a choice here!"

Sky found their gaze drifting over Rooper's shoulder to Fel Ix. He'd been so quiet this whole time, had said nothing since they released the buoy and started fleeing Dalna—where his family was.

"Fel Ix?" they said quietly.

Fel Ix looked from Sky to Rooper. "Remember your promise, Padawan."

"I do," Rooper insisted.

Sky said, "Dass, acknowledge the hyperspace coordinates. Give me two minutes, then—go."

Rooper immediately replied to her master. And Helis. "I'm here, Master Silandra. We're inputting the route now. Ready to jump in two."

"Fine," Helis said.

"Good, Rooper," Silandra Sho said.

"Master Silandra," she said, leaning toward the comm. "There is a Kessarine family on board the *Gaze Electric*. Or possibly on Dalna. Their partner Fel Ix is with me. He has helped us. His family is not our enemy. They haven't done anything wrong."

"I understand, Rooper."

Sky ignored them. They slid into the comms station and connected to the Dalna buoy that had just been inside the *Brightbird*'s hold. It answered the ping immediately.

Whole, open, public. Sky dug into the subspace frequency and triggered their algorithm. The data burst flared out along the whole network.

"Ready, Dass," they said, leaning back in the seat.

In the moments before they jumped to hyperspace, Sky just stared at the lights of the comms console.

CHAPTER THIRTY

The trip through hyperspace was quiet.

All four of the passengers on the *Brightbird* were exhausted.

They met in the galley and slumped around the table. Except for Fel Ix, who did not slump. Rooper tried not to, but her shoulders kept sinking slowly.

Sky thought this was the kind of situation where they should be celebrating or asleep. But they couldn't bring themself to leave their new friends (except for Fel Ix) and didn't feel like celebrating. Sky wanted to force the ship out of hyperspace and make Dass use the astro-resonance machine again to try to get to Planet X.

But Sky knew it wouldn't work. Dass wouldn't do it. And Rooper wouldn't let them. Sky didn't even think the machine was working properly. It hadn't been giving them coordinates that made any sense, just jumping them to other places Dass had been instead of to their goal of Planet X. Maybe Sky hadn't figured out the mechanisms of the machine yet. There was still work to do. That was the way of prospecting, after all. Guesswork and risk, and a lot of failure that might yield the right answers to put them on the path to success someday.

Besides, it was too late for this voyage. That moment had passed. Sky had made their choice to help their friends. They hoped fixing that buoy had been worth it for the Jedi and Fel Ix's family. Whatever happened on Dalna wasn't Sky's problem. Unless, of course, it became a Graf problem. Sky ground their molars. They tried not to think of their cousin Tilson Graf, who probably *had* made Dalna a Graf problem.

"Sky," Rooper said.

Sky looked at the Padawan. She seemed as tired as the rest of them, which made sense because Sky had seen that awesome move when Rooper deflected a starship's laser fire with only her lightsabers. But beyond the exhaustion, Sky saw an eagerness in Rooper's warm eyes. Probably because she was looking forward to reuniting with her master. Her hair had practically all fallen out of her braids. Rooper smiled a little. "What did you do, right at the end before we jumped?"

Dass perked up as if he hadn't realized Sky did anything. Sky wasn't sure Fel Ix was even listening.

They said, "The tech Fel Ix was using to sabotage the buoys was a Graf design. I recognized it when we fixed the buoy. I implanted a code so that when activated the buoy would pass the code and scramble the sabotage algorithms. Basically undo them, so the buoys are just buoys again. Public, or whatever." Sky pouted. They couldn't help it.

"You . . . fixed all the buoys at once?" Rooper clarified, eyes widening.

Sky shrugged.

"That's incredible!" Dass said.

"Not really." Sky pressed their hands into their eyes. "It

isn't a miracle or anything. It will only work if the buoys can communicate with each other in the first place. So they have to be on the same network, and not already shut off or on the fritz or anything. They could just be broken, like usual."

"Still." Dass reached over and patted their hand. Sky glanced at the kid, and Dass grinned. His goggles had slid farther back than usual on his head, dragging his wild hair with them, away from his face. Dass looked pretty ridiculous. Sky felt a surge of affection. Then their face fell. Aunt Jacinda would probably ship Sky off to the Grafs in the Core or lock them up on Thelj for this. Stealing the *Brightbird* and harming the Graf code in all those buoys. Even if it had been amazing and stylish. Sky hadn't even found Dad to make everything worth it.

"What's wrong?" Rooper asked.

"Doing the right thing stinks," Sky muttered.

Dass choked on a laugh. Rooper leaned closer and tentatively put her arm around Sky's shoulders. "No, it doesn't," she said gently.

"If the Path made it to Planet X," Fel Ix said suddenly, "perhaps they will have news of your father."

It was the first time they'd heard the Kessarine's rough voice in a while. They all three looked at him.

Sky didn't think Fel Ix was going to get back to his family any time soon, no matter what the Jedi promised. That was something they had in common.

"You know, both of you," Rooper said to them, "that the Force connects us all. Everything. Even far apart, you're connected to the people you love. Even things that are gone are still a part of the Force."

"I know," Fel Ix said. He glanced at Rooper for a moment, then back at the table.

Sky said, "It hurts."

"You have to let it hurt," Rooper murmured. "Let that hurt move through you. Flow around you, and onward, until you aren't carrying it anymore. Until you find peace trusting that you can always find them again through the Force."

"Maybe," Sky whispered.

Dass said, "You sound like a real Jedi, Rooper."

Rooper gasped prettily.

Dass quickly continued, "I mean, I know you're a real

Jedi—a Padawan. I mean you sound, uh, grown-up, you know?"

The Padawan nodded but seemed slightly embarrassed.

"Can they knight you for all of this?"

"I'm too young," Rooper demurred.

"That's silly, if you've done enough."

Rooper smiled gently, and they fell into silence again. Sky spaced out a bit, jerking free of it when their head bobbed like they'd almost fallen asleep.

Dass suddenly said, "I think we should all be looking forward. The Republic is going to be out here more and more. They're just as interested in connecting the galaxy and expanding hyperspace lanes as your family is, Sky."

"With everything that happened on Jedha and . . . this conflict on Dalna now," Rooper said slowly, "probably even more so."

"I'm going to get myself on a Pathfinder team," Dass said. "Not just prospecting. And I'm giving up on the *Silverstreak*. It's our past, not our future. We don't need it. If somebody else found it, okay. My mom's holo can make somebody else happy. But maybe it's all still back there, part of it. Maybe it made a mark on the planet. Maybe I'll never know."

"That's brave," Rooper said. She reached out and took Dass's hand. "I think if you talk about it with your father, he'll understand. He'll want you to pursue your skills and dreams."

"Thanks, Rooper. I . . ." Dass nodded firmly. "I want to try to explain to him. I'm going to." Dass flashed a look at Sky. "As much as I can, I'll explain. So much of this is a mystery. I . . . like a good mystery. The whole galaxy is a mystery, if you think about it. Pockets of total unknown stuff. Dangerous stuff, like monsters and that mushroom thing that almost ate me. But also stuff that can help people, or make people rich!"

Sky couldn't help smiling slightly at that.

Dass smiled back. "You have a mystery, too. Your own. It's a reason to keep going out there. Explore. Find adventure. I think it makes you stronger."

"Thanks, Dass," Sky whispered.

CHAPTER THIRTY-ONE

Within moments of docking at
Black Spire Outpost on Batuu, Rooper
found herself barely resisting throwing her arms around
Master Silandra. They met in the space between the stalls
for starships, under the open blue sky.

Instead of hugging Silandra, Rooper grinned way too
widely and offered a stuttering bow.

Master Silandra strode up to her, grasped her elbows,
and squeezed.

Silandra looked tired, which in most cases would have
been enough to give Rooper nightmares, but that day she

merely understood. Maybe Dass was right. Maybe she was growing up.

"Rooper. We have so much to discuss." Silandra eyed her. The Jedi Master's willowy frame leaned slightly over Rooper. The silver arc of her shield, lovely even when deactivated, framed her head and shoulders.

"I have plenty to tell you. Did Master Buran come with us?"

"He remained at Dalna to assist the Council. He has assured me he will do what he can to find your friend's family."

"Thank you," Rooper said. "Can you tell me anything of what did happen?"

Silandra nodded and turned, ushering Rooper back toward the *Brightbird*'s bay. "The situation has been contained. There was a skirmish of some kind on the planet, involving the Path of the Open Hand, Republic officials, and some . . ." Silandra frowned. "I cannot say. There are few reliable details at the moment."

"Monsters?" Rooper whispered, thinking of what Fel Ix had told her about the Leveler that attacked Jedi, and the rumors about Jedha.

But Master Silandra pressed her lips together. "As I said, the details are sparse, but the situation has been contained. Thanks to that buoy you repaired, I was in contact with Master Yoda on his way from Coruscant. The Jedi Council are taking care of what needs to be done on Dalna and will send us our orders here. Take me to your friends."

Waiting at the base of the boarding ramp beneath the shiny silver and black of the *Brightbird* were Dass, Sky, and Fel Ix. The Kessarine stood behind the others, as if ready to dart back into the ship at a moment's notice. Sky had their fists on their hips, their hair freshly slicked back in those black and silver stripes, and their chin up defiantly. But they kept shooting looks toward the neighboring bay, where their brother Helis's ship was in the process of docking.

Dass stepped forward and waved. "Master Silandra. I'm glad to see you."

"Young Dass Leffbruk. Your father must be worried."

"I contacted him. He's coming here from Travyx Prime." Dass scuffed his foot and told Rooper, "He had the San Tekka ship he signed on with for the Hyperspace Chase leave him there. Because he couldn't follow me, and wanted to be there in case I came back."

Rooper grimaced. Spence Leffbruk was probably going to be very, very upset. "You were brave, Dass, and smart. It'll be okay."

"I hope so."

"Just be honest with him, and he'll understand. He loves you. He'll believe you and trust you if you let him."

"Thanks, Rooper."

Master Silandra cleared her throat.

"Oh, yes, Master. This is Sky Graf, captain of the *Brightbird*, and that's Fel Ix. He's . . . well he's a member of the Path of the Open Hand. The Kessarine who helped us."

Silandra studied Fel Ix, who put his hands behind his back carefully and lowered his eyes. It made Rooper slightly uncomfortable to see him so submissive, but she remembered accusing him of being a grunt when they first met. And just because he'd helped her didn't really mean he'd given up his beliefs that the Jedi abused the Force and needed to be stopped. Or feared.

"Fel Ix," Silandra said. "I have alerted my fellow Jedi to be looking for your family. We are uninterested in causing harm to them, or to anyone in the Path who has not attacked the Republic or the Jedi. The situation is very complicated and confusing, I must admit. But I am very interested in speaking with you."

Fel Ix said nothing. Sky stepped in front of him, to Rooper's surprise. "He'll talk to you if he wants to. Fel Ix, get back on the ship."

The Kessarine's cheek furls tensed, and then he nodded and strode up the ramp. Dass said, "I'll go with him and wait for my dad."

Silandra waited for Sky to explain themself. She tapped one pale finger against her hip.

Sky paused, and Rooper could tell they were gathering courage, only because she'd spent so many days trapped in the ship with them. Finally, Sky said, "It's my ship, and he's my guest. The Jedi can't just have him."

Rooper bit her cheek to keep from smiling proudly.

Master Silandra inclined her head. "I would like to request a meeting with Fel Ix, then, Captain Graf. And to inform you that the Republic and the Jedi will be investigating the details of what happened on Dalna thoroughly. It is good that you repaired the buoy at such a critical time so that we could get our reinforcements where they needed to be. We were able to take the day. But moving forward, it would be best if we worked together. The Grafs and the Republic are quite entangled."

Sky twisted their lips. But they nodded. "Sure. I'm aware of some of the Graf involvement. But we're individuals, you know, not like the Jedi. If my cousin acted against you, it has nothing to do with me. Also . . ."

The spinning lights in the bay next to theirs slowed and stopped, and steam released as the *Starlily* completed its landing. The airlock would open very soon.

"Yes?" Silandra prompted.

"I need to speak to my brother," Sky grumbled. But then they added, "But if he tries to take my ship and claim it's his, I might tell him I can't go anywhere yet because we're working so closely with the Jedi. Okay?"

Rooper met her master's brown eyes. She nodded, hoping Silandra would agree.

Silandra paused, focused on Rooper. She seemed to see what she needed to there and told Sky, "Okay."

"I'm going to go now," Sky said. "You're welcome to talk on the *Brightbird.*"

CHAPTER THIRTY-ONE

"Thanks, Sky. Good luck. We'll see you soon." Rooper nodded.

After Sky hurried past them, Master Silandra waited again, studying Rooper. "Shall we, Padawan?"

Rooper took a deep breath. "Yes. But, Master?"

"Rooper?"

"Will you show me how you use your shield?" she asked in a rush.

"Why?"

Rooper let her gaze wander up to the blue dots tattooed on Master Silandra's forehead. They were the same color as Silandra's lightsaber blade and the plasma field of her shield when it was activated. Master Silandra had told Rooper she'd put the marks there so they could serve as a reminder of her desire to be a shield over a blade. That she was always a tool of the Force, not only its weapon.

Rooper said, "I tried to be like you, Master. I wanted to be a shield. To protect my friends, and the Force. Even though I had to use my lightsabers, even though I had to be more aggressive a few times. It was a last resort."

"I see."

"And . . ." Rooper hesitated, but Silandra waited for her

to collect her thoughts. "I thought about the nature of my relationship to the Force. I like the . . . solidity of being a shield. On behalf of the Force, and the Jedi."

Master Silandra smiled. "Very well, Padawan. I will show you how I use it when we have the space. Perhaps it will prepare you further for your trials, once you are of age."

A rush of giddy relief nearly made Rooper laugh. She reined it back into a pleased smile. "Thank you."

"Now, I'd like to speak with this Fel Ix of the Path of the Open Hand . . . and then, my Padawan, I will hear about this adventure you had."

"Of course." Rooper nodded and led Master Silandra up into the *Brightbird*. She didn't bother trying to smother her grin anymore.

CHAPTER THIRTY-TWO

Sky stomped up the ramp into Helis's borrowed ship. It was an older solar sailer retrofitted with subsidiary reactors that rendered the sails decorative antiques, but still nice. The sound of their boots rang in the hold as they entered.

Helis stopped in his tracks, halfway to Sky. The skirt of his long blue jacket actually glimmered with thick silver-and-gold embroidery. "Sky."

They clenched their jaw and tried to look defiant and in charge.

Helis crossed his arms. The siblings resembled each other, but Helis was taller and broader, and almost three years older. Still looking at Sky, he said, "Leave us," and the well-armed goon and skinny protocol droid behind him turned back into the corridor.

"There's Jedi on board the *Brightbird* now," Sky said. It was strong, as opening gambits went.

Their brother grimaced and let his head fall back. *"Sky,"* he groaned.

Sky shrugged. Their heartbeat throbbed, they were so nervous. But they didn't want to be. The blaster from the *Brightbird*'s cockpit was holstered in the small of their back. Not like they'd use it. But it was a nice weight reminding them they could.

Helis slowly sighed and looked back at them. He looked them up and down. "You look good in that flight suit."

"Thanks."

"And you're okay?"

"Yeah," they said, frowning. Why wasn't he yelling yet?

"Good. What were you thinking?" He charged forward, and for a moment Helis looked just like Dad.

Sky moved to meet him, but instead of fighting, they

threw their arms around Helis's neck and hugged him.

He caught them, but it took a moment before Helis hugged them back. His arms tightened around their ribs until the fancy chest plate of Sky's flight suit creaked.

"I was thinking about Dad," they whispered. They balanced on their tiptoes.

"Oh," Helis said into their hair.

"I wanted to find him. You weren't looking anymore. Nobody was."

Helis pulled back, and Sky let their heels hit the floor. "There was nowhere to look, Sky. Nothing to do," he said. "We would have been lost, too, if we'd kept after him. That's what prospecting is like."

"He was looking for Planet X, and I thought I had a way to get there, too." Sky fought against the way their face tightened with grief.

Helis twisted his lips like he'd tasted something sour. "That weird old tech you were working on? The copper one? With all the old scratches of whatever dead language?"

"Yeah."

"It works?"

"No. Not really. I'm not quite there yet." Sky slowly

raised their gaze to meet Helis's. "But maybe if you . . . helped me, we could figure it out together."

The siblings looked at each other for a long moment. Helis finally said, "You know . . . if Dad could, he'd have come home. Like they say, 'If you can't go forward, go back to where you started.'" It was an old hyperspace prospector saying.

"Always return home," Sky murmured. That was how their dad interpreted it. But he hadn't meant Thelj or Coruscant. He'd meant family.

"The *Brightbird* seems like a nice place for a home," Helis suggested meaningfully.

Sky snorted. "All right, Helis. Let me show you around my ship."

Their brother's eyes narrowed. "My ship."

"Ours?" Sky smiled their best innocent smile. It was unbelievable. Grafs weren't good at sharing, even with family.

"Mine," Helis insisted as he took Sky's wrist and dragged them back down the ramp. "But I'll let you pilot sometimes."

They were saying goodbye.

It had been two days since the *Brightbird* landed on Batuu, since Rooper reunited with Master Silandra and Sky with their brother. Fel Ix and Master Silandra had spent much of the time in discussions. Fel Ix had told Silandra what she wanted to know about the philosophy and history of the Path of the Open Hand. And he'd described what he knew of the interactions with Jedi on Dalna—involving the Leveler, which he insisted on calling a great balancer of the Force.

In return, Silandra had allowed Fel Ix to hear the

intelligence that came to her: the Path of the Open Hand was no more, and whatever remnants not taken into custody by the Jedi had returned to the *Gaze Electric* and vanished into hyperspace.

The Jedi did not know how to find the *Gaze*. It wasn't their priority, either, Master Silandra had admitted.

But Rok Buran would be arriving any moment, and he had the Kessarine's family with him.

Rooper sat at a small table in the Black Spire market with her friends Sky and Dass, and Fel Ix, too. They'd met there for a lunch of the root-worm wraps Sky had been wanting to try. The café was situated on a wide balcony overlooking half the market and afforded them a great view of the incoming ships at the spaceport.

Dass was in the middle of explaining—half with his mouth full—that he and his dad had had a great conversation the night before, after a really huge argument. Spence Leffbruk was still sleeping in the hostel room he'd arranged and Sky Graf insisted on paying for. "For a while, I'm going to stay with Dad, while he really gets back on his feet," Dass said with a smile. "But I'm going to help make decisions and pilot. And when I turn fifteen, he's going to let me apply to whatever pilot school I want. That's the earliest they let you in at most of them."

"I could teach you to pilot right now," Sky offered with an aggressive grin.

Dass said, "I know. I really want to, and appreciate it. But—"

"You should be with your dad," Sky answered.

"Yeah."

Fel Ix reached out and patted Dass's shoulder, though the Kessarine's gaze remained on the sky. He was obviously eager to see his own family again.

Rooper said, "I'm really happy for you, Dass. Maybe in a few years, once you're a pilot and I'm a Knight, we'll end up on the same Pathfinder team."

Dass laughed. "That would be great."

"That reminds me." Rooper sat up straight and dug into one of her utility pockets. The compass was there, where it had been for a couple of weeks, since she'd taken it from the archive at the Jedi outpost there on Batuu. She'd thought then that maybe she'd give it to Dass, only to be drawn into his adventure with Sky. Then she'd decided the compass had been a sign from the Force that she was supposed to be with them. That the Force wanted her there. And that had been so right.

"Dass." Rooper held out the compass. It fit in her palm. "This is for you. I brought it with me at the beginning of all this, and I'm even more certain now that you should take it."

Dass's round eyes widened further. "A Jedi compass? But . . . I can't use the Force."

"The Force wants you to have it."

"If you don't want it, I'll take it," Sky said, but with a tilt to their smile to show they were teasing—mostly.

Dass took the compass and held it in both hands. "It's warm."

The Force around him brightened a little, and Rooper let herself relax into it. Soon she'd have to say goodbye to them—for now. Her own small team of friends. Rooper didn't doubt she'd see them all again, if the Force willed it. And the Force connected all living things. It brought people together.

"Do you need it, though?" Dass suddenly asked Sky. "Are you going to keep looking for Planet X?"

"No," Sky said quietly. "Helis wants to get back to

Travyx Prime for the end of the Hyperspace Chase. We're leaving this afternoon, too. He misses that San Tekka girlfriend of his," Sky sneered a little. Then they sighed. "Afterwards, Helis and I are going to work on the Graf astro-resonance machine together, but Dad would have come back to us if he could. I'm not giving up or anything," Sky insisted. "We just need to sort some things out with our family first, and what we want our legacy to be, you know?"

Rooper squeezed Sky's hand.

Sky slid a sly glance her way. "And buy up all the private lanes we can out here before the Republic gets their hands on too many of them."

Before Rooper could respond, Master Silandra's tinny-sounding voice interrupted from Rooper's pocket. "Rooper."

"Master," Rooper said, raising the comlink to her mouth.

"Rok's ship is entering atmosphere. He'll be docked shortly."

Fel Ix stood, face tilted to the sky.

"Thanks, Master. We'll head back."

Rooper replaced her comlink and realized her friends

were all watching the sky with Fel Ix. So she did, too. Ships had been coming and going all morning, as it was a busy hub. But right then there was a lull, so it was easy to mark the appearance of Master Buran's ship.

The silhouette grew against the blue, and they could hear the hum of the bright engines.

Fel Ix murmured, "Excuse me," and took off.

The rest followed, moving more slowly through the crowds to the space docks. Sky teased Dass, putting their elbow on his shoulder as they walked and leaning in hard, until Dass slung his arm around Sky's waist. Rooper smiled softly and kept herself composed, as a Jedi should be.

By the time they arrived, Master Buran's ship was hissing as it settled into the stall two over from the *Brightbird*. Rooper hung back with Sky and Dass at first, while Fel Ix dashed right up to the old shuttle.

The landing gear locked into place, and almost immediately the boarding ramp blared a quick alert before lowering.

It hadn't even hit the ground before Kessarine came pouring out.

Two were as tall and lanky as Fel Ix, with green-gray

skin and scales that glinted in the daylight. Their cheek furls were coiled tight, and they wore long gray robes, with tails poking out beneath the layers. In their arms were five little babies clinging to them.

Fel Ix met them at the base of the ramp, and his partners and babies immediately folded him into a huge embrace.

Rooper's chest felt tight, but in a good way. She was glad that after everything that had happened, she got to witness this. The reunion of this family meant a lot to her. They didn't have to fight with the Path of the Open Hand, whatever was left of them. Even if they and the Jedi held disparate views, they could coexist in the galaxy. With the Force.

Fel Ix had told her he hoped to take his family back to the planet Atalia, where he'd been born, to see if they could settle there doing the kind of farming work they'd enjoyed on Dalna. Without the Path, though not without the memory of what they'd believed for so long. Fel Ix understood that the Mother had been dangerous and used the Force for her own ends. He still believed in what he'd learned about living in clarity, harmony, and freedom with the Force, but he refused to wage war over it. And he said he hoped for news of his friend Marda Ro but that such a life of extremes was not what he sought for his children.

"They're sweet," Dass said.

Sky grimaced, but agreed. "Yeah. I'm glad for them."

"Me too," said Rooper.

Before his family could bundle him away, Fel Ix paused. He carefully extracted himself from his partners' hold and handed two of the babies, who'd leapt at him, back to their other parents. He turned to Rooper and stepped toward her.

"Padawan Rooper Nitani," he said. Behind him, his partners flinched away. Fel Ix looked at them over his shoulder and said, "She is not to be feared. The Jedi are . . . not our enemy."

The other Kessarine studied her carefully as Fel Ix continued to walk toward her.

Rooper met him halfway.

Fel Ix held out his hands, palms up. "The Force will be free," he said.

Rooper smiled and touched her palms to his. She answered, "May the Force be with you."

ABOUT THE AUTHOR

Tessa Gratton is the author of award-winning adult and YA novels and short stories that have been translated into twenty-two languages. Her recent work includes the dark queer fairy tales *Strange Grace* and *Night Shine*, the YA fantasy *Chaos and Flame*, and the queer Shakespeare retellings *The Queens of Innis Lear* and *Lady Hotspur*. Her upcoming work includes more *Star Wars: The High Republic* novels for all ages. She resides at the edge of the Kansas prairie with her wife. Nonbinary. She/any. Tessagratton.com.

ABOUT THE ILLUSTRATOR

Petur Antonsson is a freelance illustrator for publishing and animation who lives in Reykjavik, Iceland. His full name is Pétur Atli Antonsson Crivello, and he was born and raised in Iceland by his Icelandic mother and French father. He graduated from the Academy of Art University in San Francisco in 2011 with a BFA in illustration. Petur worked in the gaming industry in San Francisco before moving back to Iceland, where he's currently doing freelance illustration work for various clients and companies around the world. He is represented by Shannon Associates.